D1329776

WITCHES, WIT,
and a WEREWOLF

ALSO

WITCHES, WIT,
and a WEREWOLF

Retold by Jeanne B. Hardendorff
Illustrated by Laszlo Kubinyi

J. B. LIPPINCOTT COMPANY
Philadelphia and New York

ACKNOWLEDGMENTS

From the Loom of the Dead adapted from the story of the same name and *The Grammatical Ghost* from THE SHAPE OF FEAR by Elia Wilkinson Peattie published by Macmillan, 1898.

The Witch in the Stone Boat retold from THE LEGENDS OF ICELAND by George E. J. Powell and Eirikr Magnusson printed by Robert Davis, 1866.

On the River adapted from the story of the same name by Guy de Maupassant from MODERN GHOSTS published by Harper Bros., 1890, and *Fear* adapted from story of the same name in THE WORKS OF GUY DE MAUPASSANT published by Bigelow and Smith, 1908.

Vengeance Will Come retold from *Syfaddon Lake* from THE WELSH FAIRY BOOK by W. Jenkyn Thomas published by Frederick A. Stokes, 1908.

The Questioning Ghost retold from *The Deserterer* from TALES OF WONDER by Kate Douglas Wiggin published by Doubleday, 1909.

Striking a Corpse Candle, The Power of St. Tegla's Well retold from stories of the same name from THE WELSH FAIRY BOOK by W. Jenkyn Thomas published by Frederick A. Stokes, 1908.

The Strangling Woman created from an anecdote found in LORD HALIFAX'S GHOST BOOK published by Didier, 1944.

An Imperfect Conflagration by Ambrose Bierce from his COLLECTED WORKS published by Neale, 1909.

To very special friends
The Peughs
of
Thomas Point,
Annapolis

CONTENTS

WITCHES, WIT,
and a WEREWOLF

FROM
THE
LOOM
OF
THE
DEAD

WHEN URDA BJARNASON TELLS A TALE ALL THE MEN STOP
their talking to listen, for they know her to be wise with
the wisdom of the old people. She is very old. Her
daughters and sons are all dead, but her granddaughter
says that Urda is twenty-four and a hundred, and there
are others who say that she is older still. She watches
all that the Iceland people do in the new land.

She watches yet other things. When the blue shadows
dance on the snow, Urda leaves her corner behind the
iron stove, and stands before the window, resting her
two hands on the stout bar of her cane, and gazing out
across the waste with eyes which age has restored after
four decades of decrepitude.

The young Icelandmen say:

"Mother, it is the clouds hurrying across the sky that
made the dance of the shadows."

"There are no clouds," she replies, and points to the jewellike blue of the arching sky.

"It is the drifting air," explains Fridrik Hallddersson, he who has been in the Northern seas. "As the wind buffets the air, it looks blue against the white of the snow. 'Tis the air that makes the dancing shadows."

But Urda shakes her head, and points with her dried finger, and those who stand beside her see figures moving, and airy shapes and contortions of strange things, such as are seen in a beryl stone.

"But Urda Bjarnason," says Ingeborg Christianson, "why is it we see these things only when we stand beside you and you help us to the sight?"

"Because," says Urda, with a steel-blue flash of her old eyes, "having eyes you will not see."

Not even Ingeborg can deny that Mother Urda tells true things.

"Today," says Urda, standing by the little window and watching the dance of the shadows, "a child breathed thrice on a farm at the west, and then it died."

The next week at the church gathering, when all the sledges stopped at the house of Urda's granddaughter, they said it was so—that John Christianson's wife never heard the voice of her son, but that he breathed thrice in his nurse's arms and died.

"Three sledges run over the snow, toward Milton," says Urda, "all are laden with wheat, and in one is a stranger. He has with him a strange engine, but its purpose I do not know."

Six hours later the drivers of the three empty sledges stop at the house.

"We have been to Milton with wheat," they say, "and Christian Johnson, here, carried a photographer from St. Paul."

Now it stands to reason that the farmers like to amuse themselves through the silent and white winters. And they prefer above all things to talk or to listen, as has been the fashion of their race for a thousand years. Among all the storytellers there is none like Urda, for she is the daughter and the granddaughter and the great-granddaughter of storytellers. It is given to her to talk, as it is given to John Torlaksson to sing—he who sings so as his sledge flies over the snow at night, the people come out in the bitter air from their doors to listen, and the dogs put up their noses and howl, not liking music.

In the little cabin of Peter Christianson, the husband of Urda's granddaughter, it sometimes happens that twenty men will gather about the stove. They hang their bearskin coats on the wall, put their fur gauntlets underneath the stove, where they will keep warm, and then stretch their stout, felt-covered legs to the wood fire. The room is fetid; the coffee steams eternally on the stove; and from her chair in the warmest corner Urda speaks out to the listening men. Among the many, many tales she tells is that of the dead weaver.

"Jon and Loa lived with their father and mother far to the north of the Island of Fire, and when the children looked from their windows they saw only wild scaurs and jagged lava rocks, and a distant, deep gleam of the sea. They caught the shine of the sea through an eye-

15

shaped opening in the rocks, and all the long night of winter it gleamed up at them like the eye of a dead witch. But when it sparkled and began to laugh, the children danced about the hut and sang, for they knew the bright summertime was at hand. Then their father fished, and their mother was gay. But it is true that even in the winter and the darkness they were happy, for they made fishing nets and baskets and cloth together—Jon and Loa and their father and mother—and the children were taught to read in the books, and were told the sagas, and given instruction in the part singing.

"They did not know there was such a thing as sorrow in the world, for no one had ever mentioned it to them. But one day their mother died. Then they had to learn how to keep the fire on the hearth, and to smoke the fish, and make the black coffee. And also they had to learn how to live when there is sorrow at the heart.

"They always wept together at night for lack of their mother's kisses, and in the morning they were loathe to rise because they could not see her face. The dead, cold eye of the sea watching them from among the lava rocks made them afraid, so they hung a shawl over the window to keep it out. And the house, try as they would, did not look clean and cheerful as it had used to do when their mother sang and worked about it.

"One day, when a mist rested over the eye of the sea, like that which one beholds on the eyes of the blind, a greater sorrow came to them, for a stepmother crossed the threshold. She looked at Jon and Loa, and made complaint to their father that they were still very small and not likely to be of much use. After that they had to rise earlier than ever, and to work as only those who have their growth should work, till their hearts cracked for weariness and shame. They had not much to eat, for their stepmother said she would trust to the gratitude of no other woman's child, and that she believed in laying up against old age. So she put the few coins that came to the house in a strong box, and bought little food. Neither did she buy the children clothes, though those which their dear mother had made for them were so worn that the warp stood apart from the woof, and there were holes at the elbows and little warmth to be found in them anywhere.

"Moreover, the quilts on their beds were too short for their growing length, so that at night either their purple feet or their thin shoulders were uncovered, and they wept for the cold, and in the morning, when they crept into the larger room to build a fire, they were so stiff they could not stand straight and there was pain in their joints.

"The wife scolded all the time, and her brow was like a storm sweeping down from the Northwest. There was no peace to be had in the house. The children might not repeat to each other the sagas their mother had taught them, nor try their part singing, nor make little doll cradles of rushes. Always they had to work, always they were scolded, always their clothes grew thinner.

" 'Stepmother,' cried Loa one day—she whom her mother had called the little bird—'we are a-cold because of our rags. Our mother would have woven blue cloth for us and made it into garments.'

" 'Your mother is where she will weave no cloth!' said

the stepmother, and she laughed many times.

"All in the cold and still of that night, the stepmother wakened, and she knew not why. She sat up in her bed, and knew not why. She knew not why, and she looked into the room, and there, by the light of a burning fish's tail—'twas such a light the folk used in those days—was a woman, weaving. She had no loom, and shuttle she had none. All with her hands she wove a wondrous cloth. Stooping and bending, rising and swaying with motions beautiful as those the Northern Lights make in a mid-winter sky, she wove a cloth. The warp was blue and mystical to see; the woof was white, and shone with its whiteness, so that of all the webs the stepmother had ever seen, she had seen none like to this.

"Yet the sight delighted her not, for beyond the drifting web, and beyond the weaver she saw the room and the furniture—aye, saw through the body of the weaver and the drifting of the cloth. Then she knew—as the haunted are made to know—that 'twas the mother of the children come to show her she could still weave cloth. The heart of the stepmother was cold as ice, yet she could not move to waken her husband at her side, for her hands were fixed as if they were crossed on her dead breast. The voice in her was silent, and her tongue stood to the roof of her mouth.

"After a time the wraith of the dead mother moved toward her—the wraith of the weaver moved her way— and round and about her body was wound the shining cloth. Wherever it touched the body of the stepmother, it was as hateful to her as the touch of a monster out of

18

sea-slime, so that her flesh crept away from it, and her senses swooned.

"In the early morning she awoke to the voices of the children, whispering in the inner room as they dressed with half-frozen fingers. Still about her was the hateful, beautiful web, filling her soul with loathing and with fear. She thought she saw the task set for her, and when the children crept in to light the fire—very purple and thin were their little bodies, and the rags hung from them—she arose and held out the shining cloth, and cried:

" 'Here is the web your mother wove for you. I will make it into garments!' But even as she spoke the cloth faded and fell into nothingness, and the children cried:

" 'Stepmother, you have the fever!' "

And then:

" 'Stepmother, what makes the strange light in the room?'

"That day the stepmother was too weak to rise from her bed, and the children thought she must be going to die, for she did not scold as they cleared the house and braided their baskets, and she did not frown at them, but looked at them with wistful eyes.

"By fall of night she was as weary as if she had wept all the day, and so she slept. But again she was awakened and knew not why. And again she sat up in her bed and knew not why. And again, not knowing why, she looked and saw a woman weaving cloth. All that had happened the night before happened this night. Then when the morning came, and the children crept

in shivering from their beds, she arose and dressed herself, and from her strong box she took coins, and bade her husband go with her to the town.

"So that night a web of cloth, woven by one of the best weavers in all Iceland, was in the house; and on the beds of the children were blankets of lamb's wool, soft to the touch and fair to the eye. After that the children slept warm and were at peace; for now, when they told the sagas their mother had taught them, or tried their part songs as they sat together on their bench, the stepmother was silent. For she feared to chide, lest she should wake at night, not knowing why, and see the mother's wraith."

THE
WITCH
IN
THE
STONE
BOAT

ONCE UPON A TIME THERE LIVED IN ICELAND A KING AND Queen who had an only son named Sigurd.

One day the King said to Sigurd, "It is now time for you to choose a bride. Visit first the country of my friend Hadrada for I hear his daughter is a marvel of beauty and goodness."

Sigurd set out at once on his journey taking with him several young men from his father's court. He set sail in his galley whose high prow cut through the waves while the stern with its carving and gilding glittered in the sun.

They sailed for many days and at last reached Hadrada's country at night. The moon was shining as brightly as the sun on the shore with its strange, grotesque crags and peaks. It seemed unapproachable till at last they found a large fjord. At the head of the fjord rose the King's palace.

Lights shone from every window in the palace and there was music and the sound of revelry for a banquet was being held. Sigurd and his companions went to the palace where Hadrada and his daughter Helga welcomed them.

Sigurd found the princess was as beautiful and gentle as she had been pictured and he made up his mind to win her for his bride. The next day Sigurd told King Hadrada why he had come and asked for the princess Helga's hand in marriage.

Hadrada gave his consent and Sigurd agreed to stay at Hadrada's court until such time as his father sent a message that he should return home.

So the marriage of Sigurd and Helga took place with great pomp and ceremony. In a year's time a son was born. When three years had passed, Sigurd received a message from his father saying that he was to set sail immediately, for the old King knew that his days were numbered.

The ship was made ready, Helga bade her father good-bye, and this time the viking ship rode the sun-tipped waves carrying Helga and their son Kurt and Sigurd to his native land.

For several days the wind was favorable but within one day's sail of Sigurd's country the wind stopped. Day after day the sun blazed down fierce and strong. The ship lay becalmed; not a breath of air was to be felt.

The crew went below as did Sigurd's companions and they were soon asleep in their cabins while Sigurd and Helga and young Kurt remained on deck. After a little

while a strange drowsiness seemed to overpower Sigurd himself and he said to Helga, "I can no longer stay awake; I am going below." When he reached his cabin he too fell into a deep sleep like that of the crew and his companions.

Helga was now alone on the deck with the young prince. Suddenly, she saw a strange object moving slowly along the smooth surface of the water. Shading her eyes with her hands she watched it. A monstrous large figure was working the oars of a boat.

Nearer and nearer it came, with silent swift strokes and as it touched the vessel with a hard sound Helga saw that it was very large and cut out of granite. With one spring the terrible giant-witch who had been rowing the stone boat was on deck.

As one in a dream, Helga could neither move nor utter a sound to arouse Sigurd or the ship's crew. She seemed held immobile by an invisible power. The witch came up to Helga and, snatching up the child, placed him behind her; then she removed all of Helga's beautiful embroidered robes, leaving her only the single linen garment. As the witch put on Helga's clothes, she gradually began to assume her shape and likeness. When the witch had become so like Helga, there was no telling the difference, she took Helga, put her into the stone boat and said,

"This is my speech, and this is my spell,
That never resting, thou shalt go,
Faring, to my brother, who doth dwell
Down in the worlds below."

Helga sat as if frozen, unable to move as the boat given a mighty push by the witch glided swiftly away from Sigurd's vessel and was soon out of sight.

When it was no longer to be seen, Kurt began to cry and nothing that the witch tried would make him stop. Soon losing her patience, she went down below to where Sigurd lay sleeping.

Shaking Sigurd roughly to awaken him, she began immediately to scold him for leaving her on deck alone with Kurt. "It was very thoughtless of you to leave me on the deck with no one to stand guard. There is no telling what might have happened; as it is Kurt has begun to cry without stopping and I cannot quiet him. If you and your lazy crew had been on deck, you would know that there is a wind great enough to fill the sails and we might even now be underway."

Sigurd was astonished at being spoken to by Helga in such a manner, it was so unlike her, but he did not say anything, thinking that she was overcome by the heat and the crying of the child.

After he had roused the crew and the sails had been hoisted Sigurd tried to quiet the child to no avail. With the winds filling the sails, they reached Sigurd's country the following day. In a few days time the old King died and Sigurd became king.

Strange to say that ever since the calm at sea Kurt never ceased his crying and sobbing so it was decided to turn the child over to a nurse who had come from Helga's country and indeed in her care the young prince once again became happy.

26

Sigurd was puzzled over the change that had come over Helga ever since their journey. She who had once been so kind and gentle was now obstinate, cross, and untruthful. And before long all the members of the court began to notice how disagreeable and quarrelsome the Queen was.

Now, it happened, there were at court two young men who were so devoted to playing chess that they would sit for hours in their room over the game. Their room was next to that of the Queen. Even as they played chess they were aware that there were mysterious sounds coming from the Queen's room. One day hearing her move about and talking angrily, they looked through a chink in the wall, and they heard her say,

"When I yawn slightly, I grow small and dainty like the Queen Helga; when I give a bigger yawn, I grow to half my size; when I stretch out my arms and yawn with all my might, I grow to my original size and once more become a giant-witch."

And as she said these words, she stretched herself, yawned frightfully, as if her jaws would break, and suddenly grew into an enormous giant-witch. Then, stamping her foot three times, the floor opened, and up came a three-headed giant, bearing a huge trough of raw meat. The giant, without saying a word, put the trough of meat before the witch, who set to work to empty the trough, never stopping till she had finished eating all that was in it. When she had finished eating, the giant disappeared down the same way he had come up, and the witch gave a little yawn and was once more

27

the size and likeness of the Queen Helga. The young men became frightened for the giant-witch was a terrible sight to behold and they decided to keep their own counsel about what they had seen.

That same evening when the nurse who was caring for Prince Kurt had lit the lamp and was sitting with the prince before putting him to bed, some boards in the floor suddenly burst open and through them rose a beautiful lady, dressed only in a linen garment with an iron belt around her waist. From the iron belt a chain of countless links led down into the earth as far as could be seen. The lady went silently towards the child, picked him up, embraced him lovingly, and then put the child down. After this, she disappeared, the same way she had come and the floor closed over her head.

The nurse was too frightened to speak of what she had seen to anyone. The next night the lady appeared as before and did as she had done before but this time as she was leaving she said, "Two are past; and only one is left." Then she disappeared down the same way, and the floor fell into place again.

The nurse was more frightened than she had been the first night so she went to Sigurd to tell him all that had happened. Sigurd decided that he would be in the room well before the hour that the woman with the iron belt had appeared on the previous nights. He sat half hidden by the drapes at the windows holding his sword by the hilt. Just as the woman had appeared twice before, so did she appear for the third time.

When Sigurd saw the woman, he recognized his true

wife Helga and he sprung forward from his hiding place, slashed with his sword until he broke the chain. As the chain fell through the floor down into the ground there came a great wailing and moaning, and the earth heaved and the castle was tossed as though it were a boat on a tumultuous sea.

When the noise and the movement stopped, Helga began to tell her story. She told Sigurd all that had happened on the boat when he went below to sleep, how the giant-witch had cast a spell on her and how she had assumed her shape and size by donning her embroidered robes; how she had been sent to the giant-witch's brother down below the earth; how the three-headed giant had imprisoned her and threatened to kill her if she did not consent to wed him. She told how she had at last agreed to marry him, if he would let her return on three succeeding nights to see her child.

The three-headed giant had agreed, but as a precaution he had put the iron belt around her waist and attached to it the chain which he then fastened to his own waist. She was to tell no one who she was nor why she appeared. She had finally thought of a way to draw the attention of the King to her coming. No doubt the moans and wailing as well as the violent upheaval had been the three-headed giant falling to his death for his living place was deep in the ground under the castle.

The giant-witch had reverted to her true size and the King's guards seized her. They bound her in a sack after which she was stoned to death and then her body was tied to wild horses who tore it to pieces.

Sigurd's people who had never known the real Queen were overjoyed that he had indeed married a woman fit to be Queen and not the quarrelsome, ill-tempered woman they had thought to be the Queen.

Sigurd and Helga and their son Kurt lived to a ripe old age and there was peace in the country.

ON
THE
RIVER

I HAD RENTED, LAST SUMMER, A LITTLE COUNTRY HOUSE on the banks of the Seine a few miles from Paris, and I used to go down there every night to sleep. In a few days I made the acquaintance of one of my neighbors, a man between thirty and forty, who was certainly the most curious type that I had ever met. He was an old rowing man, crazy about rowing, always near the water, always on the water, always in the water. He must have been born in a boat, and he would certainly die in a boat at last.

One night, while we were walking together along the Seine, I asked him to tell me some stories about his life upon the river; and at that the good man suddenly became animated, transfigured, eloquent, almost poetical! In his heart there was one great passion, devouring and irresistible—the river.

"Ah!" said he to me, "how many memories I have of

that river which is flowing there beside us. You people who live in streets, you don't know what the river is. But just listen to a fisherman simply pronouncing the word. For him it is the thing mysterious, the thing profound, unknown, the country of mirage and of phantasmagoria where one sees, at night, things which do not exist, where one hears strange noises, where one trembles causelessly, as though crossing a graveyard. And it is, indeed, the most sinister of graveyards—a graveyard where there are no tombstones.

"To the fisherman the land seems limited, but on dark nights, when there is no moon, the river seems limitless. Sailors have no such feeling for the Sea. Hard she often is and wicked, the great Sea; but she cries, she shouts, she deals with you fairly, while the river is silent and treacherous. It never even mutters, it flows ever noiselessly and this eternal flowing movement of water terrifies me far more than the high seas of ocean.

"Dreamers pretend that the Sea hides in her breast great blue regions where drowned men roll to and fro among the huge fish, in the midst of strange forests and in crystal grottoes. The river has only black depths, where one rots in the slime. For all that is beautiful when it glitters in the rising sun or swishes softly along between its banks where the reeds murmur.

"The poet says of the ocean:

" 'O seas, you know sad stories! Deep seas, feared by kneeling mothers, you tell the stories to one another at flood tides! And that is why you have such despairing voices when at night you come towards us nearer and nearer!'

"Well, I think that the stories murmured by the slender reeds with their little soft voices must be yet more sinister than the gloomy dramas told by the howling of the high seas.

"But, since you ask for some of my recollections, I will tell you a curious adventure which I had here about ten years ago.

"I then lived, as I still do, in the house of the old lady Lafon, and one of my best chums, Louis Bernet, who has now given up for the Civil Service his oars, his low shoes, and his sleeveless jersey, lived in the village of C——, two leagues farther down. We dined together every day—sometimes at his place, sometimes at mine.

"One evening I was returning home alone and rather tired, wearily pulling my heavy boat, a twelve-footer, which I always used at night. I stopped a few seconds to take breath near the point where so many reeds grow, down that way, about two hundred meters before you come to the railroad bridge. It was a beautiful night; the moon was resplendent, the river glittered, the air was calm and soft. The tranquillity of it all tempted me; I said to myself that to smoke a pipe just here would be extremely nice. Action followed upon the thought; I seized my anchor and threw it into the stream.

"The boat, which floated down again with the current, pulled the chain out to its full length, then stopped; and I seated myself in the stern on a sheepskin, as comfortable as possible. One heard no sound—no sound; only sometimes I thought I was aware of a low, almost insensible lapping of the water along the bank, and I made out some groups of reeds which, taller than their fellows, took on surprising shapes, and seemed from time to time to stir.

"The river was perfectly still, but I felt myself moved by the extraordinary silence which surrounded me. All the animals—the frogs and toads, those nocturnal singers of the marshes—were silent. Suddenly on my right, near me, a frog croaked. I started; it was silent. I heard nothing more, and I resolved to smoke a little by way of a distraction. But though I am, so to speak, a regular blackener of pipes, I could not smoke that night; after the second puff I sickened of it, and I stopped. I began to hum a tune; the sound of my voice was painful to me, so I stretched myself out in the bottom of the boat and contemplated the sky. For some time I remained quiet, but soon the slight movements of the boat began to make me uneasy. I thought that it was yawing tremendously, striking now this bank of the stream, and now that; then I thought that some Being or some invisible force was dragging it down gently to the bottom of the water, and then was lifting it up simply to let it fall again. I was tossed about as though in the midst of a storm. I heard noises all around me. With a sudden start I sat upright; the water sparkled, everything was calm.

"I saw that my nerves were unsettled, and I decided to go. I pulled in the chain; the boat moved. Then I was conscious of resistance. I pulled harder; the anchor did not come up, it had caught on something at the bottom of the river and I could not lift it. I pulled again—in vain. With my oars I got the boat round upstream in order to change the position of the anchor. It was no use; the anchor still held. I grew angry, and in a rage I shook the chain. Nothing moved. There was no hope of breaking the chain, or of getting it loose from my craft, because it was very heavy, and riveted at the bow into a bar of wood thicker than my arm; but since the weather continued fine, I reflected that I should not have to wait long before meeting some fisherman, who would come to my rescue. My mishap had calmed me; I sat down, and I was now able to smoke my pipe. I had a flask of brandy with me; I drank two or three glasses, and my situation made me laugh. It was very hot, so that, if needs must, I could pass the night under the stars without inconvenience.

"Suddenly a little knock sounded against the side. I started, and a cold perspiration froze me from head to foot. The noise came, no doubt, from some bit of wood drawn along by the current, but it was enough, and I felt myself again overpowered by a strange nervous agitation. I seized the chain, and I stiffened myself in a desperate effort. The anchor held. I sat down exhausted.

"But, little by little, the river had covered itself with a very thick white mist, which crept low over the water, so that, standing up, I could no longer see either the stream or my feet or my boat, and saw only the tips of the reeds, and then, beyond them, the plain, all pale in the moonlight, and with great black stains which rose towards heaven, and which were made by clumps of Italian poplars. I was as though wrapped to the waist in a cotton sheet of a strange whiteness, and there began to come to me weird imaginations. I imagined that someone was trying to climb into my boat, since I could no longer see it, and that the river, hidden by this opaque mist, must be full of strange creatures swimming about me. I experienced a horrible uneasiness, I had a tightening at the temples, my heart beat to suffocation; and, losing my head, I thought of escaping by swimming; then in an instant the very idea made me shiver with fright. I saw myself lost, drifting hither and thither in this impenetrable mist, struggling among the long grass and the reeds which I should not be able to avoid, with a rattle in my throat from fear, not seeing the shore, not finding my boat. And it seemed to me as though I felt myself being drawn by the feet down to the bottom of this black water.

"In fact, since I should have had to swim upstream at least five hundred meters before finding a point clear of rushes and reeds, where I could get a footing, there were nine chances to one that, however good a swimmer I might be, I should lose my bearings in the fog and drown.

"I tried to reason with myself. I realized that my will was firmly enough resolved against fear; but there was something in me besides my will, and it was this which felt afraid. I asked myself what it could be that I dreaded; that part of me which was courageous railed at that part of me which was cowardly; and I never had comprehended so well before the opposition between those two beings which exist within us, the one willing, the other resisting, and each in turn getting the mastery.

"This stupid and inexplicable fear grew until it be-

came a terror. I remained motionless, my eyes wide
open, with a strained and expectant ear. Expecting—
what? I did not know save that it would be something
terrible. I believe that if a fish, as often happens, had
taken it into his head to jump out of the water, it would
have needed only that to make me fall stark on my back
into a faint.

"And yet, finally, by a violent effort, I very nearly re-
covered the reason which had been escaping me. I again
took my brandy flask, and out of it I drank great
draughts. Then an idea struck me, and I began to shout
with all my might, turning in succession towards all
four quarters of the horizon. When my throat was completely paralyzed, I listened. A dog howled, a long way
off.

"Again I drank; and I lay down on my back in the
bottom of the boat. So I remained for one hour, perhaps
for two, sleepless, my eyes wide open, with nightmares
all about me. I did not dare to sit up, and yet I had a
wild desire to do so; I kept putting it off from minute to
minute. I would say to myself: "Come! get up!" and I
was afraid to make a movement. At last I raised myself
with infinite precaution, as if life depended on my
making not the slightest sound, and I peered over the
edge of the boat.

"I was dazzled by the most marvelous, the most
astonishing spectacle that it can be possible to see. It
was one of those phantasmagoria from fairyland; it was
one of those visions described by travelers returned out
of far countries, and which we hear without believing.

"The mist, which two hours before was floating over

the water, had gradually withdrawn and piled itself upon the banks. Leaving the river absolutely clear, it had formed, along each shore, long low hills about six or seven meters high, which glittered under the moon with the brilliancy of snow, so that one saw nothing except this river of fire coming down these two white mountains; and there, high above my head, a great, luminous moon, full and large, displayed herself upon a blue and milky sky.

"All the denizens of the water had awaked; the bull-frogs croaked furiously while, from instant to instant, now on my right, now on my left, I heard those short, mournful, monotonous notes which the brassy voices of the marsh frogs give forth to the stars. Strangely enough, I was no longer afraid; I was in the midst of such an extraordinary landscape that the most curious things could not have astonished me.

"How long the sight lasted I do not know, because at last I had grown drowsy. When I again opened my eyes the moon had set, the heaven was full of clouds. The water lashed mournfully, the wind whispered, it grew cold, the darkness was profound.

"I drank all the brandy I had left; then I listened shiveringly to the rustling of the reeds and to the sinister noise of the river. I tried to see, but I could not make out the boat nor even my own hands, though I raised them close to my eyes.

"However, little by little the density of the blackness diminished. Suddenly I thought I felt a shadow slipping along near by me; I uttered a cry. A voice replied—it was a fisherman. I hailed him; he approached, and I told him of my mishap. He pulled his boat alongside, and both together we heaved at the chain. The anchor did not budge. The day came on—somber, gray, rainy, cold—one of those days which bring always a sorrow and a misfortune. I made out another craft; we hailed it. The man aboard it joined his efforts to ours, then, little by little, the anchor yielded. It came up, but slowly, slowly, and weighted down by something very heavy. At last we perceived a black mass, and we pulled it alongside.

"It was the corpse of an old woman with a great stone round her neck."

VENGEANCE WILL COME

IT SO HAPPENS THAT SYFADDON LAKE WAS ONCE A BEAU-
tiful castle with much land that belonged to a great
lady.

There was once a young man from Brecon, born of
a good family but possessing no fortune, who loved the
great lady. She loved him but would not marry him
because he was poor.

He loved her beyond all measure and reason and one
night he met a rich merchant in a lonely spot away
from the village. Now the young man knew that the
merchant was carrying much gold and many gems in
a leather pouch secreted on his person—so he murdered
him.

He hastened to show the lady the gems and the gold
he had taken from his victim. He again asked her to
marry him. This time she consented.

She was curious, nonetheless, to know how he happened to have such wealth, though she did not care whether he had come by it honestly or otherwise. He told her.

"Have you buried the corpse?" she asked.

"No," said he, "I made all haste to come to you."

"You must go this night," she said, "and bury it; otherwise his kith and kin will find out someway that it was you who murdered him, and they will avenge his murder."

So the young man returned to the lonely spot where he had murdered the merchant and began to dig a grave.

While he was digging he heard a voice and the voice whispered, "Vengeance will come!"

The young man stopped his digging immediately, and looked all around him. He could see no one so he began to dig again.

Again a voice said, "Vengeance will come!" And this time the voice shouted as it spoke.

And again the young man stopped his digging to look all around, but he could see no one. He picked up his spade and commenced to dig.

And for the third time a voice from out of the darkness spoke and this time it roared like thunder, "Vengeance will come!"

This was too much for the young man and he threw down his spade and fled in terror to the great lady. He told her what he had heard.

"You must go back," she said, "and if you hear the voice again, ask when the punishment will fall."

So the young man, most reluctantly, went back to

the lonely spot where he had murdered the merchant. This time he was allowed to bury the body in peace.

Just as he finished, he heard that dreaded voice again say, "Vengeance will come!"

The young man plucked up his courage and asked, "When?"

"In the lifetime of thy grandson's great-grandson's grandson," was the answer.

The young man hurried back to the castle to tell his lady love.

"There is no reason for us to fear," said she. "We shall be dead long before that."

The murderer and the great lady felt safe enough—curse or no curse—and they were married. They had sons and daughters who in turn married and had children. These children married and the family became very numerous until at last their grandson's great-grandson's grandson was born.

By this time the murderer and the great lady were very old, but they still rejoiced in their prosperity (for they had flourished like the green bay-tree).

They said to each other, "We are rich and powerful and our family is numerous. We have lived a long life and we have lived as we liked. Let us, before we die, give a great and splendid feast to all of our family. Let us call them to us. Let us make merry, one more time, before we have to bid them good-bye."

So all the family was bid to come to the castle on a certain date. And a great and splendid feast was prepared. All the many generations of the family were

42

feasting together. There was much gaiety and mirth and at its very peak, the ground that was under the castle split asunder and the earth opened and swallowed them up—even to the grandson's great-grandson's grandson. Not one soul of them escaped and a deluge of water flooded the place.

Vengeance had come and now the place of the castle is known as Syfaddon Lake.

THE
QUESTIONING
GHOST

ONCE UPON A TIME THERE WAS A SOLDIER WHO HAD trouble in the army of the Tsar. Twice he had undergone severe punishment; the third time he knew he was face to face with death. So he resolved to flee by night and hide himself by day in some ditch or thicket, for he was afraid that in the daylight he might be recognized.

The next night, he saw a glimmer of light in the distance, and thought to himself, "I will go toward that light; perhaps it will somehow help me out of my trouble."

When, however, he came up to that light all he saw was an opening just wide enough for him to creep into. The moment he was inside thick darkness fell upon him. He could find his way neither in nor out; but on groping around he at last came upon a staircase, up which he climbed and found himself in a passageway. Through this passageway he went for a long, long time, until at last he stumbled upon a door. He opened the door and stepped into a room, but it was pitch dark there, too; so he groped all about until a last he stumbled upon another door and entered another room.

So on he went through eleven rooms, and finally reached the twelfth, where at last he found a lighted candle upon a table. The room was beautifully furnished with couches and chairs and tables, even a piano. And the soldier thought to himself, "Come what come may, I shall make myself at home in this room."

So he stretched himself upon a couch. He lay there for a while lost in thought, when, lo and behold! the table began to lay itself. When the cloth was spread, all sorts of good food and drink began to appear on it.

"Come what come may," he said to himself again, "I am hungry and I will eat and drink." So he fell to and ate to his heart's content. When he had eaten all that he could swallow, he threw himself upon the couch again and began to think.

Suddenly three women entered, clothed entirely in black. One seated herself at the piano, while the two others danced, without saying a word to the soldier. Tired as he was, when he saw this he arose and danced with the ladies. After they had stopped dancing they began to talk to the soldier, talking of one thing and another, and finally came round to the question of how he might break the spell that bound them.

They told him the very way and manner of doing it,

45

saying that he had nothing more nor less to do than to pass the night in a certain room which they would show him.

A ghost would come there and pester him with all sorts of questions—who he was, how he had come to be there and all manner of other questions. But he must not under any circumstances say a mortal word to all these questions, not though the ghost tormented him in all sorts of ways; if he could only hold out in silence the ghost would vanish, and then he would feel not the least pain from all the torments he had been enduring. Others had tried to break the spell but they had not been able to resist answering a question.

Well, the soldier thought that he could do that and so without further words, the ladies escorted him to the fateful room and left him there alone. When they were gone he undressed, bolted the door securely, and lay down on the bed. But he could not sleep, for he kept thinking about what was to happen.

At eleven o'clock a sudden knock was heard at the door. He dared not make a sound, for he was determined to ransom himself, the ladies, and the enchanted castle; so he kept still as a mouse. Again the knocking came, but he made no answer. At the third knock the door flew open, and in walked a gigantic ghost all clothed in flames.

The ghost placed himself at the bedside and began to ask the soldier who he was and why he had come; but the soldier never uttered a word. Then the ghost seized him, threw him upon the floor, and began to

torment him; but no sound passed the soldier's lips. At the stroke of twelve the ghost departed, saying:

"Though you wouldn't tell me what I asked tonight, you will tomorrow, when we all three come."

When the ghost finished speaking, the door flew open, closed again, and he was gone. The soldier arose from the floor, lay down on the bed again, and fell asleep, without feeling the least harm.

Next morning the three ladies appeared. They were all in white up to their knees, and they led him back to the room where he had been the previous day. They placed a chair for him and set a delicious breakfast before him. When he had breakfasted to his complete satisfaction he fell asleep and snored till evening.

When he awoke he asked how late it was. The ladies replied that it was nine o'clock; and they gave him a good supper and led him again to the same room to sleep.

At the stroke of eleven someone knocked at the door. He made no sound, but at the third knock the door flew open and three ghosts entered. The one who had been there the night before asked him the same questions as before, but received no answer. Then one of them seized him and flung him about until the poor fellow lay helpless against the wall, all covered with blood.

When the clock struck twelve the spokesman said to him, "Though you won't answer tonight, you will tomorrow, when we all four come." With these words the door flew open, closed again, and they disappeared.

He again lifted himself up, lay down upon his bed,

and felt no harm. In the morning the three ladies came, all in white up to their waists, and escorted him, to the sound of music, into the other room where, after breakfast, he again fell asleep.

At night they escorted him to the same room to sleep. When they were gone he did not go to bed as usual, but began to consider how he might avoid the fearful torment in store for him. He wondered if he could withstand the torture that four ghosts would inflict.

First he looked out of a window, but the look told him that below the window was a frightful abyss enclosed by rocky precipices. He went to the second window, but there it was no better, but seemed to be even worse. So nothing was left him but to heap all the furniture of the room before the door, in the hope that he might thus escape his tormentors. At eleven o'clock the knocking began. He made no answer, but at the third knock the door flew open and all the furniture returned to where it belonged in the room.

The ghost who had questioned him the other nights now began to repeat his questions, commanding him to tell who he was and how he came to be there; but the soldier was not to be made to speak. Then the ghost who was questioning him ordered one of the other ghosts to go below and bring up the anvil and four hammers, and when these had been brought, one of the ghosts blew up a fire and threw the soldier upon it. When he was heated to a glow, they laid him upon the anvil and beat him with hammers until he was flat as paper. But with all of this he did not speak one word or make one sound.

The time was up and ghosts must go for the clock was striking midnight. Before they went they told him that he and all around him were blessed; and then the door flew open and they vanished. He again arose, laid himself upon the bed, and sank at once into sleep.

Next morning the three ladies, all in white from head to foot, came to thank him for ransoming them, and they told him to choose among them for a wife. Now the youngest of them had grown nearest to his heart, and he declared himself ready to marry her.

And so he married the youngest of the three ladies with great festivities. As they came out of the church to go to their house, a new city sprang up along the roadside. The rejoicing was great.

STRIKING
A
CORPSE
CANDLE

THERE WAS ONCE A SON OF A CLERGYMAN IN WALES WHO came home one night very late. He found all the doors of the house locked.

He did not wish to disturb his father and mother, so he went to the man-servant's quarters over the stable.

He could not wake the man-servant, but while he was standing by his bed he saw a small flame come from the man's nostrils. It was a corpse candle.

Curious, the young man followed the light. It went over a footbridge, which crossed a brook, and on to the road which led up to the church.

After following the corpse candle for some time, the young man, just to see what would happen, struck at it with his stick.

The corpse candle burst into sparks, but afterwards, reunited into a flame again as before. The flame then floated on until it finally disappeared inside the church-yard.

Not long afterwards the man-servant died. As the men were carrying the bier with the coffin to the cemetery in the churchyard, the bier broke at the very spot where the young man had struck the corpse candle with his stick and the coffin fell to the ground.

THE
STRANGLING
WOMAN

ONE TUESDAY TOWARDS THE END OF OCTOBER, ROBERT
Eastwood, the portrait painter, received a letter from
a Mr. and Mrs. Albert Gordon. The Gordons asked the
artist if he would consider painting the portraits of
their daughters. In order that he might meet the daughters and decide if he would accept the commission,
they invited him to visit them that very weekend at
their place in the country.

Robert Eastwood felt that a visit to the country would
be a very pleasant change and he had heard many tales
about the Gordons' old house. The house was nearly
four hundred years old and as yet had neither electricity
nor a telephone. So he wrote to say that he would take
the four-fifteen train on Friday from London.

By the time Robert Eastwood arrived the house was
filled with unexpected company. And when it came
time to tell the artist which was to be his room, he

noticed that there was a mysterious sort of muttering between his hosts. He could not hear everything that was said between Mr. and Mrs. Gordon but he did hear Mr. Gordon say, "It cannot be helped; there is no other!"

Robert Eastwood wondered what his room would be like but when he found it was neither damp nor cold as he had feared, he thought no more about it.

After a very late dinner, everyone went immediately to his room. Robert Eastwood went to bed at once and it seemed to him that he had scarely closed his eyes when something waked him. He looked around his room and he saw a strange sight.

In the moonlight he could see standing at the foot of his bed an old woman. She was wringing her hands and she seemed to be searching the floor around his bed for some lost object. And she kept saying over and over, "Where is it? Oh, where is it? I mustn't leave it!"

At first Robert Eastwood thought she was a guest and he thought, too, she had somehow or other mistaken his room for her own. So he sat up in bed and said,

"I beg your pardon, madam, but you are in the wrong room."

The old woman made no reply but, as soon as the artist spoke and to his great surprise, she just disappeared. One second she was there and in the next she was gone.

"Hmmm," said Robert Eastwood to himself as he lay down, "if ever there was a ghost, that is one."

Next morning when he went down to breakfast, Mrs. Gordon asked if he had slept well. He noticed an anxious look on her face as though she dreaded to hear his reply.

"Oh, I slept very well, thank you, but I did have a very strange visitor." And then he told about the old woman who had appeared in his room. He told how she had stood at the foot of his bed, wringing her hands, and as soon as he spoke she had disappeared.

"I was afraid that you might see her, since we were so late going to bed," said Mr. Gordon. "We try never to use that room if we can avoid it for many of our guests have been terrified by the apparition of that woman. Now that you have seen her, I shall tell you about her.

"It seems that she committed a murder in that room. She isn't an ancestor of ours, but she did at one time own this house. In fact, she inherited this house by murdering the heir to it. The heir was a boy of seven who was not too strong nor any too well, but as long as he lived, he would keep her from inheriting this house. So one day she sent the child's nurse away on some errand and then she murdered the boy in such a way no one ever suspected that she had been the cause of his death. So clever had she been, no one would have ever known about it if she had not confessed to it as she was dying. To this day no one knows how she managed to do it, nor what she used. When the property was sold after her death, my grandfather bought it and our family has lived in this house for over a hundred years."

"Do you think she will appear again?" Robert Eastwood asked.

"Certainly," Mr. Gordon replied. "She will return and she will return about the same time of night—of that you can be sure. She has done so ever since she died."

Robert Eastwood had decided that he would paint the daughters' portraits and he began to work on them as soon as he finished breakfast.

That evening after dinner when everyone was ready to go to his room, Robert Eastwood chose a lamp, in place of a candle he had used the previous night. When he reached his room, he left the lamp burning as low as possible and he placed a sketching pad and several pencils with their points sharpened on the bedside table.

He got into bed as though he were going to sleep, but he was determined to keep awake to see if the woman would reappear. He did not have long to wait for the ghost appeared as it had the night before. She again stood at the foot of his bed wringing her hands and she again appeared to be searching for some lost object as she said over and over again, "Where is it? Oh, where is it? I must not leave it!"

Robert Eastwood sat up in bed and said, "Pardon me, madam, I am an artist and I would like to make a sketch of you."

But as soon as he spoke, the ghost disappeared as she had the night before.

The next night he left the lamp burning as low as possible, and he had everything at hand to make a sketch, so when the ghost appeared he did not speak, but silently sat up in bed and began to draw. This he did each night that he stayed at the house.

The night before he was to leave, he finished drawing the ghost and after comparing what he had drawn with the figure standing at the foot of his bed, he decided that he would add, for a dramatic touch, a particular devious strangling device that he had once seen in a museum. So he drew the device, putting it in the woman's hands.

After he had added the device to his sketch, he held the drawing at arm's length, turning it this way and that so that the light from the lamp might shine on the drawing from different angles.

Robert Eastwood was so used to the ghost standing at the foot of his bed wringing her hands that he paid no attention to her so he did not notice that she saw what he had done. Nor did he notice the startled look on her face.

Satisfied with the sketch, he put the pad on his bedside table, turned out the lamp, and went to sleep.

When he awoke the next morning, Robert Eastwood found that his sketch pad had fallen onto the floor. He picked it up to take downstairs in order to show the Gordons the sketch he had made of their ghost.

After breakfast he opened his pad to show the sketch of the ghost, but it was gone. All that was left in the pad was a narrow strip of paper where a page had been torn out.

The ghost had found what she had been searching for for over one hundred years—the strangling device—so she took it and the drawing and was seen no more.

AN

IMPERFECT

CONFLAGRATION

EARLY ONE JUNE MORNING IN 1872, I MURDERED MY
father—an act which made a deep impression on me
at the time. This was before my marriage, while I was
living with my parents in Wisconsin. My father and I
were in the library of our home, dividing the proceeds
of a burglary which we had committed that night.
These consisted of household goods mostly and the
task of equitable division was difficult. We got on very
well with the napkins, towels and such things, and the
silverware was parted pretty nearly equally, but you
can see for yourself that when you try to divide a
single music box by two without a remainder you will
have trouble. It was that music box which brought
disaster and disgrace upon our family. If we had left it
my poor father might now be alive.

It was a most exquisite and beautiful piece of work-
manship—inlaid with costly woods and carven very

curiously. It would not only play a great variety of tunes, but would whistle like a quail, bark like a dog, crow every morning at daylight whether it was wound up or not, and break the Ten Commandments. It was this last-mentioned accomplishment that won my father's heart and caused him to commit the only dishonorable act of his life, though possibly he would have committed more if he had been spared: He tried to conceal that music box from me, and declared upon his honor that he had not taken it, though I knew very well that, so far as he was concerned, the burglary had been undertaken chiefly for the purpose of obtaining it.

My father had the music box hidden under his cloak; we had worn cloaks by way of disguise. He had solemnly assured me that he did not take it. I knew that he did, and knew something of which he was evidently ignorant; namely, that the box would crow at daylight and betray him if I could prolong the division of the profits till that time. All occurred as I wished: As the gaslight began to pale in the library and the shape of the windows was seen dimly behind the curtains, a long cock-a-doodle-doo came from beneath the old gentleman's cloak, followed by a few bars of an aria from *Tannhäuser,* ending with a loud click. A small hand-axe, which we had used to break into the unlucky house, lay between us on the table; I picked it up. The old man seeing that further concealment was useless took the box from under his cloak and set it on the table. "Cut it in two if you prefer that plan," said he. "I tried to save it from destruction."

He was a passionate lover of music and could himself play the concertina with expression and feeling.

I said: "I do not question the purity of your motive: it would be presumptuous in me to sit in judgment on my father. But business is business, and with this axe I am going to effect a dissolution of our partnership unless you will consent in all future burglaries to wear a bell-punch."

"No," he said, after some reflection, "no, I could not do that; it would look like a confession of dishonesty. People would say that you distrusted me."

I could not help admiring his spirit and sensitiveness; for a moment I was proud of him and disposed to overlook his fault, but a glance at the richly jewelled music box decided me and, as I said, I removed the old man from this vale of tears. Having done so, I was a trifle uneasy. Not only was he my father—the author of my being—but the body would be certainly discovered. It was now broad daylight and my mother was likely to enter the library at any moment. Under the circumstances, I thought it expedient to remove her also, which I did. Then I paid off all the servants and discharged them.

That afternoon I went to the chief of police, told him what I had done, and asked his advice. It would be very painful to me if the facts became publicly known. My conduct would be generally condemned; the newspapers would bring it up against me if ever I should run for office. The chief saw the force of these considerations; he was himself an assassin of wide experience. After consulting with the presiding Judge of the Court of Variable Jurisdiction he advised me to conceal the bodies in one of the bookcases, get a heavy insurance on the house and burn it down. This I proceeded to do.

In the library was a bookcase which my father had recently purchased of some crank inventor and had not filled. It was in shape and size something like the old-fashioned "wardrobes" which one sees in bedrooms without closets, but opened all the way down, like a woman's night-dress. It had glass doors. I had recently laid out my parents and they were now rigid enough to stand erect; so I stood them in this bookcase, from which I had removed the shelves. I locked them in and tacked some curtains over the glass doors. The inspector from the insurance office passed a half dozen times before the case without suspicion.

That night, after getting my policy, I set fire to the house and started through the woods to town, two miles away, where I managed to be found about the time the excitement was at its height. With cries of apprehension for the fate of my parents, I joined the rush and arrived at the fire some two hours after I had kindled it. The whole town was there as I dashed up. The house was entirely consumed, but in one end of the level bed of glowing embers, bolt upright and uninjured, was that bookcase! The curtains had burned away, exposing the glass doors, through which the fierce, red light illuminated the interior. There stood my dear father "in his habit as he lived," and at his side the partner of his joys and sorrows. Not a hair of them was singed, their clothing was intact. On their heads and throats the injuries which in the accomplishment of my designs I had been compelled to inflict were conspicuous. As in the presence of a miracle, the people were silent; awe and terror had stilled every tongue. I was myself greatly affected.

Some three years later, when the events herein related had nearly faded from my memory, I went to New York to assist in passing some counterfeit United States bonds. Carelessly looking into a furniture store one day, I saw the exact counterpart of that bookcase. "I bought it for a trifle from a reformed inventor," the dealer explained. "He said it was fireproof, the pores of the wood being filled with alum under hydraulic pressure and the glass made of asbestos. I don't suppose it is really fireproof—you can have it at the price of an ordinary bookcase."

"No," I said, "if you cannot warrant it fireproof I won't take it,"—and I bade him good morning.

I would not have had it at any price: it revived memories that were exceedingly disagreeable.

THE
LITTLE
TOE
BONE

"GOOD MORNING, MR. TIGER," SAID THE LITTLE BOY VERY politely. Then he went on playing a pretty little song on his reed pipe.

"Good morning," growled the big Tiger, much surprised, for really he was just about to swallow the little boy. "You are a very polite little boy, I see, so I'll give you a choice. Would you rather I'd eat you or all your sheep?"

"Would you mind if I ask my aunt? She takes care of me, and these are her sheep. I watch them every day, and I think I ought to do just as she wishes me to, don't you?" asked the little boy very politely. Then he went on playing the pretty little song on his reed pipe.

"You are a very polite little boy, I see, so I'll wait till you ask your aunt. Does she live far away?" growled the Tiger, looking rather hungry.

"Oh, yes, she lives far away in the village, and I must not drive the sheep home until sunset; but I'll tell you the very first thing in the morning, Mr. Tiger," said the little boy very politely. Then he went on playing the pretty little song on his reed pipe.

When he reached home that evening he called, "Oh, Aunt, may I please ask you a question?"

"Well, and what is it?" snapped his aunt.

"If a big, big Tiger should come out of the jungle and ask, 'Shall I eat you or the sheep?' which should I tell him to eat?"

"Why, you, *of course*," snapped his aunt.

So next morning, when the big, big Tiger came out of the jungle and said, "Well, little boy, shall I eat you or all of your sheep?" The little boy answered, very politely, "Me, *of course*, Mr. Tiger." But the little boy did not play any pretty little song on his reed pipe.

Then the big, big Tiger looked at the little boy, and he coughed, and he switched his tail; then he looked away up to the tiptop of the tree, then he looked away off into the jungle, but he did not seem in a very great hurry to eat the little boy.

"If you please, Mr. Tiger, if you must eat me I wish you'd do it right away, for it isn't any fun to wait," said the little boy very politely.

"You're a very polite little boy," said the Tiger, "and I don't like to eat you at all, but I must live. Is there anything I can do for you after I eat you?"

"Yes," said the little boy. "After you've eaten me and picked all my bones very clean, will you lay them in a nice, tidy pile at the foot of this tree, and will you take my little toe bone and tie it up in the very tiptop of the tree?"

"Certainly I will," said the Tiger, and he did, just so.

When the winds blew, the little toe bone rocked and swung on the topmost branch, and the little white bones lay in a nice, tidy pile at the foot of the tree. And the little toe bone would go "click, click" against the branch whenever the wind blew.

One night five robbers stopped there to divide the money they had stolen. They sat under the tree, and began to count out the gold and silver into five piles. Then the little toe bone in the tiptop of the tree began to rock and swing harder than ever. And it went "click, click, click, click" against the branch of the tree. The tree began to fling its branches about, and the wind whistled by. Soon black clouds covered the stars, and the rain came down in torrents. The lightning flashed, the thunder roared, and right in the worst of the storm the little toe bone dropped from the tree right on top of the chief robber's head.

"Oh, help!" he cried. "The sky is falling on us to punish us! Let us run! Let us run!"

Away they ran through the jungle, leaving all their silver and gold in piles under the trees.

Then the storm stopped, and the stars shone again. The little toe bone rolled from off the robber's head right upon the tidy pile of little white bones, and they had turned into the little boy once more, and there he sat, playing a pretty song on his reed pipe.

FEAR

IN THE DARKNESS OF THE NIGHT THE TRAIN RUSHED ON-
ward at express speed. Seated opposite to me was an
old gentleman who was gazing out of the window; we
were the only ones in the car.

The night was suffocating, moonless, without a breath
of air, and not a star was visible. The steam from the
plunging engine came to us through the open window,
and threw into our faces a warm, sluggish breath—op-
pressive and stifling.

We had started from Paris three hours ago and were
en route for the center of France, but so far, we had
seen nothing of the country we were traveling through.
We were sitting silently by the window when suddenly
there appeared before our eyes a fantastic apparition:
before a great fire in a wood two men were standing.
We saw them for a moment only—two miserable out-
casts in tattered garments, crimson in the gleaming

light reflected from the roaring fire, their dark, bearded faces turned towards us, and round and about them, like the setting of a drama, the green trees—glimmering with rugged trunks lit up by the fiery reflex of the flames, the green foliage crossed, imbued, and steeped, by the light which crept through it.

We passed, and all became black again. It was a strange, weird vision. What were these two wretches doing in the forest? Why had they lit a tremendous fire on a sultry, suffocating night?

The old man pulled out his watch and, turning to me, remarked: "Sir, it is just midnight. That is a singular thing we have just seen."

I fully agreed with him, and we discussed the subject, trying to solve the mystery. Who could these men be, were they criminals who had waited till midnight to burn the proof of their crime? Were they wizards preparing a philter? It was not likely that anyone would light such a fire in the middle of the night—a sultry summer night—to boil soup. What were they doing then? We could not imagine, it would forever remain a mystery to us.

The man began to talk, but I could not learn from his conversation what his profession was. He was an old man, decidedly original, intelligent, and well educated, but he seemed to me to be slightly demented. However, why should I say that, for how can we distinguish between the sane and insane in this world, where madness is often called genius, and reason is called folly?

"I am glad that I saw that," he remarked, "for I felt for a few minutes a weird sensation. Do you not think that it must have been very exciting in the olden times when all was so mysterious? Tell me, do you not think that the nights are empty and the blackness of night is ordinary and common now that we no longer have apparitions? We have no more strange beliefs, we do not believe in the fantastical. Why? Because all that was unexplainable is now explainable. The supernatural ebbs away like a lake that is drained by a canal; does not science from day to day extend the limits of the marvelous?

"I must tell you, sir, that I belong to an old race, who like to hold to certain beliefs—a simple race who did not seek to fathom the mysteries of life; they did not comprehend, neither did they wish to comprehend. They would have refused the simple and plain truth. I tell you we have taken away from the imagination of man in suppressing the invisible. The world today seems to me like an abandoned sphere—empty and bare.

"When I go out at night I wish I could shudder with the fright that makes old women cross themselves as they walk quickly by the cemetery, and run away and hide when queer vapors arise from the swamps, and when they see the fantastic will-o'-the-wisp. I wish I could believe in that something so vague and terrifying, which they imagine passes close to them at dusk. In olden times, the obscurity of the night was somber and menacing, fabulous beings, prowlers, and evil-doers groped about in the dark, their forms could not be distinguished, but the fear of them froze the marrow in the bones, their occult power passed the limits of our thoughts. With the vanishing of the belief in the supernatural, actual terror has also disappeared, for really we experience only real terror for things which we do not understand. Dangers that we see can disturb, trouble and alarm us, but is that fear compared with the convulsions conveyed to the soul by the certainty that we shall meet a ghost, that we see it gliding towards us, and that we shall soon be locked in the deadly embrace of a wandering phantom?

"The shades of nights do not seem to me to be dark now that they are no longer haunted. For example—if we suddenly found ourselves alone in the woods, we should be pursued by the image of the two strange beings who appeared before us in the blood red light of their fire, far more than by a fear of some known or real danger." And then he said again, "We experience real terror only for the things which we do not understand."

I told the old man of an experience that a friend of mine had, while swimming one summer. He had tramped all day through the woods and towards the end of the afternoon he threw himself down on the banks of a river, thoroughly exhausted. The river glided calmly under the trees—clear, cool, and deep. He decided to go into the water and as he was gently drifting with the river he suddenly felt a hand placed on his shoulder and he turned with a start and faced a hideous creature. It bore partly the resemblance to a woman and partly to a gorilla. My friend was seized with a ghastly terror, the icy fear of the supernatural; without thinking, or without a purpose or understanding, he began to swim desperately towards the shore, but the monster swam after him and came up quickly beside him; she stretched her hand and touched his neck, his back, his legs; at each touch she gave a little gurgle of delight. He learned eventually that it was a poor mad woman who had lived in the woods for thirty years but he said that nothing in his life had terrified him so much, because he did not understand what the monster was.

The old man had listened attentively. "It is true," he said, "one has only absolute terror for that which one does not understand. We can really experience the awful convulsions of the soul which we call terror, only when there is mingled with the fright a superstitious fear. I once felt this terror in all its horror.

"I was on a walking tour in Brittany. I was alone. I had crossed Finstere and tramped miles through lonely parts, across uncultivated soil where only the wild furze grew beside the huge sacred stones which the peasants believed were haunted. The day before I had explored the sinister Pointe du Raz, that bit of the old world where the two seas—the Atlantic and the Channel combat for eternity. My mind was full of legends, of stories that I had read or had heard on the subject of beliefs and superstitions. I was on my way from Penmarch to Pont-l'Abee at night. At Penmarch the seashore is flat, quite flat, and low; it almost seems as though it were lower than the sea. On all sides is the broad expanse of the ocean, graying and menacing; you can see huge slimy rocks which seem to have the form of wild beasts.

"I had dined in a little wineshop that was frequented by fishermen; as soon as I finished my meal I started on my journey, taking the right of the road which lay between two high lands. The night was very dark. As I passed the druidical stones, which looked like phantoms lowering above me, it seemed as though they turned to look at me, and little by little a vague, unreasonable fear possessed me. Fear of what? I could not tell, it was a nameless fear that was creeping slowly upon me. There are nights when one can almost feel the light touch of spirits, when the soul is chilled without reason, and the heart beats quickly under a confused uneasiness.

"The road was long—interminably long and empty. Except for the roaring of the sea which lay behind me, there was not a sound; sometimes the dreary and menacing noise seemed to be so near that I thought the water must be upon me, and I was seized with a desire to fly, to run from it at full speed. A low wind began to blow in squalls, it made the wild furze shake and softly hiss around me. I thought I would quicken my step for I was cold—deadly cold, a mortal chill of terror penetrated my body. Ah! If I could have met some human being! It was so dark that it was difficult for me to see the road before me.

"Suddenly I heard in the distance which stretched beyond, a rumbling noise. A carriage, I thought. I listened for a moment, but the noise had ceased. I could hear nothing but the sound of the waves. A minute passed and I heard again a rolling noise, but much nearer. I could not see any lights coming towards me, this struck me as being very strange. How could anyone drive

through this desolate and wild country without lanterns? I listened again, all was silent, the rolling had stopped, and then it came on again. It could not be a cart or a heavy vehicle, the noise was too light, and how was it I could not hear the horses' hoofs?

"I began to wonder at that.

"What could it be? It came towards me quickly, with increasing speed, but still I could hear only the rolling, no sound of hoofs or of feet—nothing.

"What could it be? It was quite near to me now, it was almost upon me. With a feeling of instinctive fear I leaped aside into the ditch and then there passed before my startled eyes a large wheelbarrow—alone.

"There was no one pushing it. It went on and on, at a great rate along the dark road. My heart beat so violently that I sank down among the weeds and listened to the rumbling as it died away in the distance, it was going on towards the sea. I could not move, I could not walk, for I knew that if it had returned and followed me I should have died of terror.

"It was a long time before I gained sufficient courage to continue my journey. I walked along the rest of the road with such fear at my heart, that the slightest sound made me shake and hold my breath. You will say it was foolish, but I was afraid.

"In thinking it over later, when I had fully regained my composure, I solved the mystery. Without the slightest doubt a barefooted small child was guiding it, and I was looking for the head of a man at an ordinary height. In a measure you can understand what I felt.

My mind had been dwelling on things supernatural, and along comes a barrow which was rolling onward with no visible hand to guide it.

"What a horror!"

THE
GRAMMATICAL
GHOST

THERE WAS ONLY ONE POSSIBLE OBJECTION TO THE DRAW-ing room, and that was the occasional presence of Miss Carew; and only one possible objection to Miss Carew. And that was, that she was dead.

She had been dead twenty years, as a matter of fact and record, and to the last of her life sacredly preserved the treasures and traditions of her family, a family bound up—as it is quite unnecessary to explain to any one in good society—with all that is most venerable and heroic in the history of the Republic. Miss Carew never relaxed the proverbial hospitality of her house, even when she remained its sole representative. She continued to preside at her table with dignity and state, and to set an example of excessive modesty and gentle decorum to a generation of restless young women.

It is not likely that having lived a life of such irreproachable gentility as this, Miss Carew would have the bad taste to die in any way not pleasant to mention in fastidious society. She could be trusted to the last, not to outrage those friends who quoted her as an exemplar of propriety. She died very unobtrusively of an affection of the heart, one June morning, while trimming her rose trellis, and her lavender-colored print was not even rumpled when she fell, nor were more than the tips of her little bronze slippers visible.

"Isn't it dreadful," said the Philadelphians, "that the property should go to a very, very distant cousin in Iowa or somewhere else on the frontier, about whom nobody knows anything at all?"

The Carew treasures were packed in boxes and sent away into the Iowa wilderness; the Carew traditions were preserved by the Historical Society; the Carew property, standing in one of the most umbrageous and aristocratic suburbs of Philadelphia was rented to all manner of folk—anybody who had money enough to pay the rental—and society entered its doors no more.

But at last, after twenty years, and when all save the oldest Philadelphians had forgotten Miss Lydia Carew, the very, very distant cousin appeared. He was quite in the prime of life, and agreeable and unassuming. With him were two maiden sisters, ladies of excellent taste and manners, who restored the Carew china to its ancient cabinets, and replaced the Carew pictures upon the walls, with additions not out of keeping with the elegance of these heirlooms. Society, with a magnanimity almost dramatic, overlooked his name of Boggs—and called.

All was well. At least, to an outsider all seemed to be

well. But, in truth, there was a certain distress in the old mansion, and in the hearts of the well-behaved Misses Boggs. It came about most unexpectedly.

The sisters had been sitting upstairs, looking out at the beautiful grounds of the old place, and marveling at the violets which lifted their heads from every possible cranny about the house, and talking over the cordiality which they had been receiving by those upon whom they had no claim, and they were filled with amiable satisfaction. Life looked attractive. They had often been grateful to Miss Lydia Carew for leaving their brother her fortune. Now they felt even more grateful to her. She had left them a Social Position—one, which even after twenty years of disuse, was fit for use.

They descended the stairs together, with arms clasped about each other's waists, and as they did so presented a placid and pleasing sight. They entered their drawing room with the intention of brewing a cup of tea, and drinking it in calm sociability in the twilight. But as they entered the room they became aware of the presence of a lady, who was already seated at their tea table, regarding their old Wedgwood with the air of a connoisseur.

There were a number of peculiarities about this intruder. To begin with, she was hatless, quite as if she were a habitué of the house, and was costumed in a prim lilac-colored lawn of the style of two decades past. But a greater peculiarity was the resemblance this lady bore to a faded daguerrotype. If looked at one way, she was perfectly discernible; if looked at another, she went out in a sort of blur. Notwithstanding this comparative invisibility, she exhaled a delicate perfume of sweet lavender, very pleasing to the nostrils of the Misses Boggs, who stood looking at her in gentle and unprotesting surprise.

"I beg your pardon," began Miss Prudence, the younger of the Misses Boggs, "but—"

But at this moment the daguerrotype became a blur, and Miss Prudence found herself addressing space. The Misses Boggs were irritated. They had never encountered any mysteries in Iowa. They began an impatient search behind doors and portieres, and even under sofas, though it was quite absurd to suppose that a lady recognizing the merits of the Carew Wedgwood would so far forget herself as to crawl under a sofa.

When they had given up all hope of discovering the intruder, they saw her standing at the far end of the drawing room critically examining a watercolor marine. The elder Miss Boggs started towards her with stern decision, but the little daguerrotype turned with a shadowy smile, became a blur and an imperceptibility.

Miss Boggs looked at Miss Prudence Boggs.

"If there were ghosts," she said, "this would be one."

"If there were ghosts," said Miss Prudence Boggs, "this would be the ghost of Lydia Carew."

The twilight was settling into blackness, and Miss Boggs nervously lit the gas while Miss Prudence ran for other teacups, preferring, for reasons superfluous to mention, not to drink out of the Carew china that evening.

The next day, on taking up her embroidery frame,

Miss Boggs found a number of old-fashioned cross-stitches added to her own stitches. Prudence, she knew, would never have degraded herself by taking a cross-stitch, and the parlormaid was above taking such a liberty. Miss Boggs mentioned the incident that night at a dinner given by an ancient friend of the Carews.

"Oh, that's the work of Lydia Carew, without a doubt!" cried the hostess. "She visits every new family that moves to the house, but she never remains more than a week or two with anyone."

"It must be that she disapproves of them," suggested Miss Boggs.

"I think that's it," said the hostess. "She doesn't like their china, or their fiction."

"I hope she'll disapprove of us," added Miss Prudence.

The hostess belonged to a very old Philadelphian family, and she shook her head.

"I should say it was a compliment for even the ghost of Miss Lydia Carew to approve of one," she said severely.

The next morning, when the sisters entered their drawing room there were numerous evidences of an occupant during their absence. The sofa pillows had been rearranged so that the effect of their grouping was less bizarre than that favored by the Western women; a horrid little Buddhist idol with its eyes fixed on its abdomen, had been chastely hidden behind a Dresden shepherdess, as unfit for the scrutiny of polite eyes; and on the table where Miss Prudence did work in water-colors, after the fashion of the impressionists, lay a prim and impossible composition representing a moss rose and a number of heartsease, colored with that caution which modest spinster artists instinctively exercise.

"Oh, there's no doubt it's the work of Miss Lydia Carew," said Miss Prudence, contemptuously. "There's no mistaking the drawing of that rigid little rose. Don't you remember those wreaths and bouquets framed, among the pictures we got when the Carew pictures were sent to us? I gave some of them to an orphan asylum and burned up the rest."

"Hush!" cried Miss Boggs, involuntarily. "If she heard you, it would hurt her feelings terribly. Of course, I mean—" and she blushed. "It might hurt her feelings—but how perfectly ridiculous! It's impossible!"

Miss Prudence held up the sketch of the moss rose.

"That may be impossible in an artistic sense, but it is a palpable thing."

"Bosh!" cried Miss Boggs.

"But," protested Miss Prudence, "how do you explain it?"

"I don't," said Miss Boggs, and left the room.

That evening the sisters made a point of being in the drawing room before the dusk came on, and of lighting the gas at the first hint of twilight. They didn't believe in Miss Lydia Carew—but still they meant to be beforehand with her. They talked with unwonted vivacity and in a louder tone than was their custom. But as they drank their tea even their utmost verbosity could not make them oblivious to the fact that the perfume of sweet lavender was stealing insidiously through the room. They tacitly refused to recognize this odor and all that it indicated, when suddenly, with a sharp crash, one of the old Carew teacups fell from the tea table to the floor and was broken. The disaster was followed by what sounded like a sigh of pain and dismay.

"I didn't suppose Miss Lydia would ever be as awkward as that," cried the younger Miss Boggs, petulantly.

"Prudence," said her sister with a stern accent, "please try not to be a fool. You brushed the cup off with the sleeve of your dress."

"Your theory wouldn't be so bad," said Miss Prudence, half laughing and half crying, "if there were any sleeves to my dress, but, as you see, there aren't," and then Miss Prudence had something as near hysterics as a healthy young woman from the West can have.

"I wouldn't think such a perfect lady as Lydia Carew," she ejaculated between her sobs, "would make herself so disagreeable! You may talk about good breeding all you please, but I call such intrusion exceedingly bad taste. I have a horrible idea that she likes us and means to stay with us. She left those other people because she did not approve of their habits or their grammar. It would be just our luck to please her."

"Well, I like your egotism," said Miss Boggs.

However, the view Miss Prudence took of the case appeared to be the right one. Time went by and Miss Lydia Carew still remained. When the ladies entered their drawing room they would see the little ladylike daguerrotype revolving itself into a blur before one of the family portraits. Or they noticed that the yellow sofa cushion, toward which she appeared to feel a peculiar antipathy, had been dropped behind the sofa upon the floor; or that one of Jane Austen's novels, which none of the family ever read, had been removed from the book shelves and left open upon the table.

"I cannot become reconciled to it," complained Miss Boggs to Miss Prudence. "I wish we had remained in Iowa where we belong. Of course I don't believe in the thing! No sensible person would. But still I cannot become reconciled."

But their liberation was to come, and in a most unexpected manner.

A relative by marriage visited them from the West. He was a friendly man and had much to say, so he talked all through dinner, and afterward followed the ladies to the drawing room to finish his gossip. The gas in the room was turned very low, and as they entered Miss Prudence caught sight of Miss Carew, in company attire, sitting in upright propriety in a stiff-backed chair at the extremity of the room.

Miss Prudence had a sudden idea.

"We will not turn up the gas," she said, with an emphasis intended to convey private information to her sister. "It will be more agreeable to sit here and talk in this soft light."

Neither her brother nor the man from the West made any objection. Miss Bogg and Miss Prudence, clasping each other's hands, divided their attention between their corporeal and their incorporeal guests. Miss Boggs was confident that her sister had an idea, and was willing to await its development. As the guest from Iowa spoke, Miss Carew bent a politely attentive ear to what he said.

"Ever since Richards took sick that time," he said briskly, "it seemed like he shed all responsibility." (The Misses Boggs saw the daguerrotype put up her shadowy head with a movement of doubt and apprehension.)

"The fact of the matter was, Richards didn't seem to scarcely get on the way he might have been expected to. (At this conscienceless split to the infinitive and misplacing of the preposition, Miss Carew arose trembling perceptibly.)

"I saw it wasn't no use for him to count on a quick recovery—"

The Misses Boggs lost the rest of the sentence, for at the utterance of the double negative Miss Lydia Carew had flashed out, not in a blur, but with mortal haste, as when life goes out at a pistol shot!

The man from the West wondered why Miss Prudence should have cried at so pathetic a part of his story:

"Thank goodness!"

And their brother was amazed to see Miss Boggs kiss Miss Prudence with passion and energy.

It was the end. Miss Carew returned no more.

THE
POWER
OF
ST.
TEGLA'S
WELL

AT THE FARM OF AMNOD BELL, AT THE FOOT OF LITTLE Arenig, there once lived a farmer called Robert Williams, his wife Mari, and their only child William.

Now William was subject to fits, and in the summer when he was twelve, his father and his mother became terribly anxious about him, because it happened that so many signs of death appeared to them, one after the other.

First the apple tree burst into bloom long before its time and as everyone knew that was a very unlucky sign.

Next the old cock which had behaved as well as any cock in the county took to crowing in the very middle of the night and had to have his head chopped off to break him of the habit.

Then Mari dreamed that she was at a wedding, which

of course meant that before long she would attend a funeral. For dreams go by contraries.

Then one night a bird flapped its wings against the window of the room in which Robert Williams and his wife Mari slept, and their hearts sank at the thought that it might have been the Corpse Bird, that weird, featherless bird, with wings of some leathery substance like those of a bat, which occasionally comes from the land of Illusion. It comes to beat its wings against the windows of the houses which the King of Terrors is about to visit.

Several nights later Robert Williams was so frightened by what he saw as he was walking home by himself from the fair at Bala that it was all he could do to get home at all. He was walking on that part of the road which runs alongside the River Trywern when he saw in the fading light a repulsive hag, clad in a long black gown which trailed on the ground. Her face was deadly pale, with high cheekbones and deep-sunk, lifeless eyes; from her mouth projected great large teeth all dark with decay and her nose seemed to be no more than the gaping sockets like those in a skull. Her hair was gray and tangled. Her arms were skinny and shriveled and of unusual length for they were out of all proportion to her body.

When Robert Williams saw her, she was splashing in the water of the river with her hands, and she was making a doleful noise.

At first he could not make out any of the words, but soon he could hear most clearly and he heard her moaning, "My child, my child, my dear son." Suddenly as she had appeared, she disappeared. She vanished into nothingness.

Robert Williams felt sure that he had seen the much dreaded Cyhiraeth, and that her cry foreboded the death of his only son. His blood froze in his veins and darkness closed in before he could drag himself toward home.

If seeing the dreaded Cyhiraeth was not enough for one night, he had one more sight to see before he reached his home.

He had not gone far when he saw a corpse candle moving before him along the road. It burned with a red flame and it was small. Such a corpse candle was that of a child and Robert Williams felt that all the signs he had seen pointed to only one thing. And that was the death of his only son, William.

So the very next day he went to see a wise man who lived nearby. He asked if there was any hope for his son after he told the wise man all that had happened. He asked the wise man if there was anything that could be done.

The wise man told him that his only chance and hope was to take his son to St. Tegla's Well and instructed him in what he was to do.

Robert Williams took his son to St. Tegla's Well and then the boy did as he was told.

The boy went to the well after sunset, carrying a cock in a basket. First he walked around the well three times, saying his prayers. Then he walked three times around the church, again saying his prayers.

After this he entered the church, crept under the

altar, and slept there until the break of day.

In the morning he placed sixpence on the altar and left the cock in the church and then went home with his father.

They waited anxiously to learn the fate of the cock; for if the cure was to work, the boy's ill luck should transfer to the cock.

In a week, a messenger brought the word that all had gone as was needed to affect the cure.

Whether this was so or not, it is curious that in spite of all the signs to the contrary—the apple tree which bloomed before its time, the night-crowing cock, the Corpse Bird flying against the window, the sight of the ugly old hag as well as the corpse candle—Robert Williams' son William lived to a ripe old age.

THE
WITCH
AT
FRADDAM

THERE WAS ONCE A WITCH AT FRADDAM WHO WAS THE most powerful woman in the west of England and she became very angry with the Lord of Pengerswick for his magic was stronger than hers. Try as she might, she could wreak no havoc for the Lord of Pengerswick was able to reverse her spells no matter how potent they were.

So the witch at Fraddam, by special incantations, called up the devil. She told the devil about the Lord of Pengerswick; how he and his lady had come from no one knew where and how they had built a great castle in three nights with other than human hands and a great and strong castle it was where none had been before.

She told the devil how if she set out to spoil the harvest, the Lord of Pengerswick made the harvest even better; how if she worked a spell to keep the moon from shining so that she could work a particular magic in the dark of the moon, the Lord of Pengerswick made the moon shine even brighter than was its usual wont. She complained loud and long to the devil that she had not been able to work any of her magic since the Lord of Pengerswick came to Cornwall and she wished to be rid of him.

So the devil told her what to do; for it was known far and wide that the Lord of Pengerswick rode a mare who was as docile as a lamb with its master and as wild as a lion to all other persons and that the Lord of Pengerswick rode out each night along a certain lane.

The witch at Fraddam was to place a tub of poisoned water beside the road and the mare would be tricked into drinking from the tub. One swallow of the water would so madden the mare that she would fling the Lord of Pengerswick to the ground. He would be stunned by the fall. Then the witch was to pour over the Lord of Pengerswick some hell-broth brewed in the darkest night, under the most evil position of the stars. If the witch would do this, the Lord of Pengerswick would be in her power forever and she might torment him as she pleased.

So the witch at Fraddam set about making her preparations as the devil had instructed her. First she collected with the greatest of care all the deadly things needed to brew her hell-broth. In the darkest of nights, in the midst of the wildest of storms, with the flashing of lightning and the bellow of thunder, the witch was seen riding her ram-cat over the moors and mountains as she collected the poisons.

Before long all was ready; the horse-drink was boiled and the hell-broth was brewed.

So in March, near the time of the equinox, the night was dark and a mighty storm was raging. The witch placed her tub by the roadside and she sat near the tub placing beside her the crock containing the hell-broth.

She did not have long to wait—soon she could see the outline of the Lord of Pengerswick riding his mare. On they came; the witch could scarcely keep herself hidden, so pleased was she thinking that soon she would have the Lord of Pengerswick in her power.

On came the horse and rider; they neared the tub of horse-drink; the mare snorted, and her eyes flashed fire as she smelled the evil drink in the tub.

The Lord of Pengerswick bent over the mare's neck and whispered into her ear; the mare quickly turned around and flung out her heels. With one kick she upset the tub and drink. The tub flew before the blow; it knocked against the crock which overturned. As the crock overturned it struck against the legs of the witch causing her to fall into the tub which immediately assumed the shape of a coffin.

The witch was terrified. She had planned to put the Lord of Pengerswick into her powers but instead she found herself in the tub which was now shaped like a coffin.

The Lord of Pengerswick raised his voice and spoke some wild words in an unknown tongue, at which even the mare trembled. The tub with the terrified, helpless witch inside rose into the air and the crock followed.

When the tub with the witch was high in the air, the

Lord of Pengerswick spoke again in an unknown tongue at which the tub ceased to rise and then he said to himself in a satisfied tone, "She is settled till the day of doom." And then he turned his mare around and rode rapidly home.

To this day the witch at Fraddam floats up and down over the seas, around the coast of Cornwall, in her coffin followed by the crock. She still works some mischief with her magic by roiling up the seas.

But the Lord of Pengerswick has only to stand on his tower, blow three blasts on his trumpet, to bring the witch to shore and compel her to quieten the waves.

A

WEREWOLF

OR

A

THIEF?

THERE WAS ONCE A THIEF WHO PUT UP AT A CERTAIN INN and remained there for several days. He was waiting for a chance to practice his profession. He waited and waited for something to come along that he might steal.

Finally, one day, he noticed that the innkeeper had bought himself a handsome new cloak. It was a magnificent cloak—made of the finest materials, decorated with silver threads and gold buttons. As it was a holiday, the innkeeper put on his new cloak and sat outside his inn by the door.

As there was no one in sight, the thief sat down by the innkeeper and began to talk. He talked first about this and then about that. After they had talked for some time, the thief all of a sudden yawned, and then howled—awoooooo—like a wolf.

The innkeeper was very surprised at the man's behavior and naturally asked the reason for such behavior.

"Well," answered the thief, "now that you've asked, I'll tell you, but first, I want you to promise me something."

The innkeeper said, "What do you want me to promise?"

And the man said, "Promise me, no matter what happens, that you will keep my clothes for me. It is very important. I am going to leave them here with you."

"What do you mean, 'No matter what happens'?" asked the innkeeper.

"I don't know why it is, sir," replied the thief, "that I'm attacked by these peculiar yawning spells—which are always followed by my howling like a wolf. But I do know that after I have yawned three times, I turn into a wolf—one of the man-eating sort."

Having said that, the thief yawned a second time and howled—awoooo—like a wolf again just as he had done before.

The innkeeper looked at the man and he thought about what the man had said and what he had asked him to promise and he rose up quickly for he was afraid. He started into the inn. But the thief clutched the innkeeper by his magnificent new cloak and said,

"Wait a minute, sir. I wish to give you my clothes. I don't want to lose any of them for if I do, I won't be able to turn back into a man once I've been a werewolf." And the thief made as if to unbutton his coat with his free hand, for he was still clutching the innkeeper's cloak with one hand.

Whereupon, the innkeeper was even more afraid than he had been before. In a panic, thinking he might be eaten up, the innkeeper ran into his inn and locked the door, leaving his magnificent new cloak behind him.

Thus it was that the thief by pretending that he would turn into a werewolf, managed to steal the innkeeper's new cloak.

MORAL: Don't believe everything you hear.

CAPTAIN MURDERER

IF WE ALL KNEW OUR OWN MINDS (IN A MORE ENLARGED sense than the popular acceptation of that phrase), I suspect we should find our nurses responsible for most of the dark corners we are forced to go back to, against our wills.

The first diabolical character who intruded himself on my peaceful youth was a certain Captain Murderer. This wretch must have been an offshoot of the Bluebeard family, but I had no suspicion of the consanguinity in those times. His warning name would seem to have awakened no general prejudice against him, for he was admitted into the best society and possessed immense wealth.

Captain Murderer's mission was matrimony, and the gratification of a cannibal appetite with tender brides. On his marriage morning, he always caused both sides of the way to church to be planted with curious flowers;

and when his bride said, "Dear Captain Murderer, I never saw flowers like these before. What are they called?" he answered, "They are called Garnish for House-lamb," and laughed at his ferocious practical joke in a horrid manner, disquieting the minds of the noble bridal company, with a very sharp show of teeth, then displayed for the first time.

He made love in a coach and six, and married in a coach and twelve, and all his horses were milk-white horses with one red spot on the back which he caused to be hidden by the harness. For, the spot *would* come there, though every horse was milk-white when Captain Murderer bought him. And the spot was young bride's blood. (To this terrific point I am indebted for my first personal experience of a shudder and cold beads on the forehead.)

When Captain Murderer had made an end of feasting and revelry, and had dismissed the noble guests, and was alone with his wife on the day month after their marriage, it was his whimsical custom to produce a golden rolling-pin and a silver pie-board. Now, there was this special feature in the Captain's courtships, that he always asked if the young lady could make pie-crust; and if she couldn't by nature or education, she was taught.

Well. When the bride saw Captain Murderer produce the golden rolling-pin and silver pie-board, she remembered this, and turned up her laced-silk sleeves to make a pie. The Captain brought out a silver pie-dish of immense capacity, and the Captain brought out flour and butter and eggs and all things needful, except the inside of the pie; of materials for the staple of the pie itself, the Captain brought out none.

Then said the lovely bride, "Dear Captain Murderer, what pie is this to be?"

He replied, "A meat pie."

Then said the lovely bride, "Dear Captain Murderer, I see no meat."

The Captain humorously retorted, "Look in the glass."

She looked in the glass, but still she saw no meat, and then the Captain roared with laughter, and suddenly frowning and drawing his sword, bade her roll out the crust.

So she rolled out the crust, dropping large tears upon it all the time because he was so cross, and when she had lined the dish with crust and had cut the crust all ready to fit the top, the Captain called out, "*I* see the meat in the glass!" And the bride looked up at the glass, just in time to see the Captain cutting her head off; and he chopped her in pieces, and peppered her, and salted her, and put her in the pie, and sent it to the baker's, and ate it all, and picked the bones.

Captain Murderer went on in this way, prospering exceedingly, until he came to choose a bride from two twin sisters, and at first didn't know which to choose. For, though one was fair and the other dark, they were both equally beautiful. But the fair twin loved him, and the dark twin hated him, so he chose the fair one.

The dark twin would have prevented the marriage if she could, but she couldn't. However, on the night before it, much suspecting Captain Murderer, she stole out and climbed his garden wall, and looked in at his window through a chink in the shutter, and saw him having his teeth filed sharp. Next day she listened all day, and heard him make his joke about the house-lamb.

And that day month, he had the paste rolled out, and cut the fair twin's head off, and chopped her in pieces, and peppered her, and salted her, and put her in the pie, and sent it to the baker's, and ate it all, and picked the bones.

Now, the dark twin had had her suspicions much increased by the filing of the Captain's teeth, and again by the house-lamb joke. Putting all things together when he gave out that her sister was dead, she divined the truth, and determined to be revenged.

So, she went up to Captain Murderer's house, and knocked at the knocker and pulled at the bell, and when the Captain came to the door, said: "Dear Captain Murderer, marry me next, for I always loved you and was jealous of my sister."

The Captain took it as a compliment, and made a polite answer, and the marriage was quickly arranged. On the night before it, the bride again climbed to his window, and again saw him having his teeth filed sharp. At this sight she laughed such a terrible laugh at the chink in the shutter, that the Captain's blood curdled, and he said: "I hope nothing has disagreed with me!" At that, she laughed again, a still more terrible laugh, and the shutter was opened and search made, but she was nimbly gone, and there was no one.

Next day they went to church in a coach and twelve,

and were married. And that day month, she rolled the pie-crust out, and Captain Murderer cut her head off, and chopped her in pieces, and peppered her, and salted her, and put her in the pie, and sent it to the baker's, and ate it all, and picked the bones.

But before she began to roll out the paste she had taken a deadly poison of a most awful character, distilled from toads' eyes and spiders' knees; and Captain Murderer had hardly picked her last bone, when he began to swell, and to turn blue, and to be all over spots, and to scream. And he went on swelling and turning bluer, and being more all over spots and screaming, until he reached from floor to ceiling and from wall to wall; and then, at one o'clock in the morning, he blew up with a loud explosion.

At the sound of it, all the milk-white horses in the stable broke their halters and went mad, and then they galloped over everybody in Captain Murderer's house (beginning with the family blacksmith who had filed his teeth) until the whole were dead, and then they galloped away.

RAP!

RAP!

RAP!

ON A VERY DARK AND MOONLESS NIGHT LAST DECEMBER, Reginald Ewing Peabody was driving his car very slowly and most carefully on that particular road in the southwest corner of the county which goes by the three houses which have been deserted for so many years.

He was driving very slowly for he was having trouble seeing the road. His headlights were very dim and it was obvious to Reginald Ewing Peabody that something was drastically wrong with the battery of his car. That road goes up hill and down hill with great monotony when it isn't curving first this way and that way. The road is narrow and the hedges have grown tall and close to the road—all of which add to the difficulties of driving along that particular road—late at night.

Reginald Ewing Peabody was on that road as it was a shorter route than the main highway to the house where he was expected to spend the night. He had passed two of those deserted houses a long way back, it seemed to him, and he had not passed nor seen another car for miles.

His headlights were growing dimmer and dimmer. The night was growing darker and darker. His car had just reached the crest of a hill when there was a flash of lightning followed by the pelting of rain against the windshield. At this onslaught of nature the battery, which Reginald Ewing Peabody had begun to think of as having human characteristics (he had been talking to it, urging it along, pleading and cajoling with it not to abandon him in his need), took that very instant to give up the ghost—it went completely dead.

And there was Reginald Ewing Peabody miles from any village. He had seen the outline of a house over to his left when the flash of lightning lessened the blackness of the night for a moment.

He needed some shelter from the storm; for his car was old and far from waterproof. He thought that it was possible that there might be someone living in that house and that he might be able to telephone the nearest garage. So he buttoned his slicker, turned up the collar, and made a run for the house.

At the road there was a gate which creaked and moaned as he opened and shut it. The bricks in the walk were slippery with the rain and seemed to be covered with moss as though no one had walked on them for quite some time. But he thought he had noticed a light upstairs.

He knocked on the door. But all he heard was the echo of his knock. So he knocked again. No one seemed to be coming to answer the door.

He tried the doorknob. It turned in his hand and the door opened. Reginald Ewing Peabody called out, "Anyone home?"

No answer.

The only sound he heard was a faint rap, rap, rap. And the sound was coming from upstairs.

So Reginald Ewing Peabody stepped into the front hall. He called again, "Anyone home?"

No answer. Only the sound rap, rap, rap, and it was definitely coming from upstairs. Reginald Ewing Peabody lit a match so that he could see to climb the stairs. The match burned until he reached the upstairs landing and then it went out.

He could hear the rap, rap, rap, but it was louder. So he lit another match and he went down the hall towards the sound.

Rap, rap, rap. The sound led Reginald Ewing Peabody past one door, past a second door until he came to a third door.

The sound was coming from behind that third door.

Rap, rap, rap.

Reginald Ewing Peabody opened the door. Behind the door were some stairs. The stairs led up to the attic. So he lit another match.

He climbed the attic steps and all the time the rap, rap, rap, was getting louder and louder.

Reginald Ewing Peabody stepped onto the attic floor. He looked all around the attic. He could hear the

rapping sound. At last he noticed a door. The rapping sound was coming from behind that door.

He had taken three steps towards the door, when his match burnt out; so he lit another match.

Rap, rap, rap, the sound was getting louder.

Reginald Ewing Peabody reached the door and he opened it.

Rap! Rap! Rap!

He looked in the closet.

Rap! Rap! Rap!

On the shelf of the closet was a box. The rapping sound was coming from the box.

Reginald Ewing Peabody opened the box. Inside was a roll of wrapping paper.

THE
BLOOD-DRAWING
GHOST

THERE WAS A YOUNG MAN IN THE PARISH OF DRIMALEGUE,
County Cork, who was courting three girls at one time,
and he didn't know which of them would he take; they
had equal fortunes, and any of the three was as pleasing
to him as any other. One day when he was coming home
from the fair with his two sisters, the sisters began:

"Well, John," said one of them, "why don't you get
married. Why don't you take either Mary, or Peggy, or
Kate?"

"I can't tell you that," said John, "till I find which of
them has the best wish for me."

"How will you know?" asked the other.

"I will tell you that as soon as any person will die in
the parish."

In three weeks' time from that day an old man died.
John went to the wake and then to the funeral. While
they were burying the corpse in the graveyard John

stood near a tomb which was next to the grave, and when all were going away, after burying the old man, he remained standing a while by himself, as if thinking of something; then he put his blackthorn stick on top of the tomb, stood a while longer, and on going from the graveyard left the stick behind him. He went home and ate his supper.

After supper John went to a neighbor's house where young people used to meet in the evening, and the three girls happened to be there that time. John was very quiet, so that finally everyone noticed how quiet he was.

"What is troubling you this evening, John?" asked one of the girls.

"Oh, I am missing my beautiful blackthorn," said he.

"Did you lose it?"

"I did not," said John; "but I left it on the top of the tomb next to the grave of the man who was buried to-day, and whichever of you three will go for it is the woman I'll marry. Well, Mary, will you go for my stick?" asked he.

"Faith, then, I will not," said Mary.

"Well, Peggy, will you go?"

"If I were without a man forever," said Peggy, "I wouldn't go."

"Well, Kate," said he to the third, "will you go for my stick? If you go I'll marry you."

"Stand to your word," said Kate, "and I'll bring the stick to you."

"Believe me, that I will," said John.

Kate left the company behind her, and went for the

stick. The graveyard was three miles away and the walk was a long one. Kate came to the place at last and made out the tomb by the fresh grave. When she had her hand on the blackthorn a voice called from the tomb:

"Leave the stick where it is and open this tomb for me."

Kate began to tremble and was greatly in dread, but something forced her to open the tomb—she couldn't help herself.

"Take the lid off now," said the dead man when Kate had the door open and was inside the tomb, "and take me out of this. Take me on your back."

Unable to refuse, and afraid besides, she took the lid from the coffin, raised the dead man on her back, and walked on in the way he directed. She walked about the distance of a mile. The load, being very heavy, nearly broke her back and was killing her. She walked half a mile farther and she came to a village; the houses were at the side of the road.

"Take me to the first house," said the dead man.

She took him to the first house.

"Oh, we cannot go in here," said he, when they came near. "The people have clean water inside, and they have holy water, too. Take me to the next house."

So she took him to the next house.

"We cannot go in there," said he, when she stopped in front of the door. "They have clean water, and they have holy water, too. Take me to the next house."

She took him to the third house.

"Go in here," said the dead man. "There is neither

clean water nor holy water in this place; we can go inside."

They went into the house.

"Bring a chair now and put me in the chair at the side of the fire. Then find something to eat and to drink."

She placed him in a chair by the hearth, searched the kitchen cupboards, found a dish of oatmeal, and brought it to the dead man.

"There is nothing but dirty water to drink," she said.

"Bring me a dish and razor."

She brought the dish and the razor.

"Come, now," said he, "carry me to the room above."

So she carried him to the room above, where three young men, sons of the man of the house, were sleeping, Kate had to hold the dish while the dead man drew their blood.

"Let the father and mother have that," said he, "in return for the dirty water." He closed their wounds in such a way that there was no sign of a cut on them. "Mix this now with the oatmeal, get a dish of it for yourself and another for me."

Kate got two plates and put the oatmeal in it after mixing it, and brought two spoons. She wore a handkerchief on her head; she put this under her neck and tied it; while she was pretending to eat, she was actually putting the food in the handkerchief till her plate was empty.

"Have you your share eaten?" asked the dead man.

"My plate is empty," answered Kate.

"I'll have mine finished this minute," said he, and

soon after he gave her his empty dish. She put the dishes back in the dresser after she finished washing them.

"Come, now," said the dead man, "take me back to the place where you found me."

"Oh, how can I take you back; you are too great a load; it almost killed me when I carried you here."

"You are stronger after eating that oatmeal than you were when you came; take me back to my grave."

She went against her will. She rolled up the oatmeal in the handkerchief. There was a deep hole in the wall of the kitchen by the door, where the bar was slipped in when they barred the door; into this hole she put the handkerchief. In going back to the graveyard she shortened the distance by going through a big field. When they were at the top of the field she asked, was there any cure for those young men whose blood he had drawn?

"There is no cure," said he, "but one. If any of that food had been spared, three bits of it in each young man's mouth would bring them to life again, and they'd never know of their death."

"Then," said Kate to herself, "that cure is to be had."

"Do you see this field?" asked the dead man.

"Certainly, I do," said Kate. "Am I not walking through it this very minute?"

"Well there is as much gold buried in it as would make rich people of you and all your kinfolk. Do you see the three piles of small stone? Underneath each pile of them is a pot of gold."

The dead man looked around for a while; then Kate

111

went on till she came to the wall of the graveyard, and just then they heard the cock crow.

"The cock is crowing," said Kate. "It's time for me to be going home."

"It is not time yet," said the dead man. "That is a ghost cock."

A moment after that another cock crowed. "There, the cocks are crowing a second time," said she.

"No," said the dead man, "that is a ghost cock again; that's no true bird."

They came to the mouth of the tomb and a cock crowed the third time.

"Well," said the girl, "that must be the right cock."

"Ah, my girl, that cock has saved your life for you. But for him I would have had you with me in the grave forevermore, and if I had known that true cock would crow before I was in the grave with you, you wouldn't have the knowledge you have now of the field and the gold. Put me into the coffin where you found me. Take your time and settle me well. I cannot meddle with you now, and 'tis sorry I am to part with you."

"Will you tell me who you are?" asked Kate.

"Have you ever heard your father or mother mention a man called Edward Derrihy or his son Michael?"

"It's often I've heard tell of them," replied the girl.

"Well, Edward Derrihy was my father; I am Michael. That blackthorn that you came for tonight to this graveyard was the lucky stick for you, but if you had had any thought of the danger that was before you, you wouldn't have come, I warrant. Settle me carefully and close the tomb well behind you."

Kate placed the dead man in the coffin carefully, closed the door behind her, took the blackthorn stick, and went on home. The night was almost over when she reached home. She was tired, and good reason she had. She thrust the stick into the thatch above the door of the house and knocked. Her sister opened the door and let her in.

"Where did you spend the night?" asked the sister. "Mother will kill you in the morning for spending the whole night from home."

"Go to bed," answered Kate, "and never mind what will happen to me."

They went to bed, and Kate fell asleep the minute she touched the bed—she was that tired after carting the dead man into the village and back to the graveyard.

When the father and mother of the three young men rose the next morning, and there was no sign of their sons, the mother went to the room to call them, and there she found the three dead. She began to screech and wring her hands. She ran to the road screaming and wailing.

All the neighbors crowded around to know what troubled her. She told them that her three sons were lying dead in their beds. Very soon the report spread in every direction. When Kate's father and mother heard it they hurried off to the house of the dead men. When they got back home Kate was still in bed; the mother took a stick and began to beat the girl for being out all night and staying in bed all day.

"Get up now, you lazy stump of a girl," said the mother, "and go to the wake-house; your neighbor's three sons are dead."

Kate took no notice of this. "I am tired and sick," said she. "Spare me and give me something to eat and drink."

The mother gave her a drink of milk and a bite to eat, and in the middle of the day Kate got up.

"It's a shame and a disgrace that you haven't gone to the wake-house yet," said the mother. "Hurry over now."

When Kate reached the house there was a great crowd of people before her and there was much wailing. Kate did not join in the crying and the wailing, she just looked on. The father was going up and down in front of the house wringing his hands, crying and wailing.

"Be quiet," said Kate to the father. "Control yourself."

"How can I do that, my dear girl, and my three fine sons lying dead in the house?"

"What would you give," asked Kate, "to the person who would bring life to them again?"

"Don't be vexing me," said the father.

"It's neither vexing you I am nor trifling," said Kate. "I can put the life in them again."

"If it was true that you could do that, I would give you all that I have inside the house and outside as well."

"All I want from you," said Kate, "is the eldest son to marry and the field with the three piles of small stones as a fortune."

"My dear, you will have that from me with the greatest blessing."

"Give me the field in writing from yourself, whether the son will marry me or not."

He gave her the field in writing. She told all who were inside the wake-house to go outside the door, every man and woman of them. Some were laughing at her and more were crying, thinking that Kate had lost all her senses.

Kate bolted the door inside, and went to the place where she left the handkerchief, found it, and put three bites of the oatmeal mixed with blood in the mouth of each young man, and as soon as she did that the three got their natural color, and they looked like men sleeping. She opened the door, then called on all to come inside, and told the father to go and wake his sons.

He called each one by name, and as they woke they seemed very tired after their night's rest; they put on their clothes, and were greatly surprised to see all the people around.

"Why are all the people here?" asked the eldest son.

"Don't you know of anything that came over you in the night?" asked the father.

"We do not," said the sons. "We remember nothing at all since we fell asleep last evening."

The father then told them everything, but they could not believe it. Kate went home and told her father and mother about what had happened to her the night before—about going to the graveyard, the dead man, and everything.

Later that day she met John.

"Did you get the stick?" asked he.

"Find your own stick," said she, "and never speak to me again in your entire life."

In a week's time she went to the house of the three

young men, and said to the father, "I have come for what you promised me."

"You'll get that with my blessing," said the father. He called the eldest son aside then and asked would he marry Kate.

"I will," said the son.

Three days after that the two were married and had a fine wedding. For three weeks they enjoyed a pleasant life without toil or trouble; then Kate said, "Come with me tomorrow and I'll give you and your brothers and my own father and brothers something to do."

She took them to the field with the piles of small stones. "Throw the stones to one side," said she.

They thought that Kate had lost her senses, but she told them they'd soon see for themselves why she wanted that done. They went to work and kept at it till they had dug a hole six feet deep; then they found a flat stone three feet square with an iron hook in the middle of it.

"There must be something under that stone," said the men. They lifted the stone and under it was a pot of gold. All were happy then.

"There is more gold yet," said Kate. "Come to the other pile of stones."

They did the same as before to the second pile of stones and the third pile of stones. On the side of the third pot of gold was an inscription, and they could not make out what it was. After they emptied the pot, they placed the pot beside the front door.

About a month later a poor scholar passed through the village and he stopped at the house with the pot.

As he was going in the door the pot caught his eye. He picked up the pot and began to study the letters on its side.

"You must be a good scholar if you can read what's on that pot," said Kate's husband.

"I can," said the poor scholar, "and here it is for you. 'There's a great deal more lying to the south of each pot.'"

Kate's husband said nothing, but putting his hand in his pocket paid him a good wage for the reading of the writing. When he was gone they went to work and found a great deal more gold lying to the south of each pile of stones.

They were very happy and very rich, and they bought several farms and built fine houses. They supposed that the money had been the dead man's but they never knew for sure. When they died they left property enough so that their children were rich to the seventh generation.

THE
THREE
SHEEP

ONCE UPON A TIME THERE WERE THREE SHEEP, WHO lived on a high rock. One day one of them said: "Brothers, I don't like this rock. I shall go somewhere where the grass grows green and the pools are full of wine."

"Very well," said his brothers.

So he climbed down off the high rock onto the plain, and he ran across the plain like the wind, and when seven days and seven nights had passed he came to an ivory castle, and at the door of the castle stood a knight all in armor.

"Sheep," said the knight, "where are you going?"

"I am looking for a place where the grass grows green and the pools are full of wine," said the sheep.

"Then come in with me," said the knight. And he drew from a bag that he carried seven ribands: one was red, and one was blue, and one was yellow, and one was orange, and one was purple, and one was green, and one was white; and he bound the seven ribands round the neck of the sheep and led him into the castle. When they passed through the courtyard they came into a great hall, where sat a king feasting, and his throne was all of scarlet wood.

"Sir King," cried the knight, "I bring with me a sheep, who seeks a place where the grass grows green and the pools are filled with wine."

"Then he, too, must wait," said the king.

Then the sheep looked about him and saw a long table where sat every kind of beast and man; there were white men and black men and yellow men, Frenchmen and Spaniards and Chinamen, and pigmies and Germans and English; there were elephants and lions, and a hippopotamus and a goat and a horse and a unicorn and a weasel, a cat and a great brown bear; and each sat more still than the others.

Then the knight led the sheep by his seven ribands to an empty seat. And he sat there a day, a month, and a year, he sat there two years: and at the end of a hundred years a trumpet blew and a beautiful maiden walked into the castle.

"O King, I ask a boon," she cried.

"Speak on, damsel," said the king.

"Give me a man or a beast," said the damsel.

So the sheep rose up, and she caught hold of his seven ribands and led him out into the night.

"Where are you taking me?" asked the sheep.

"I am taking you across seven continents and seven seas," answered the maiden.

So they ran like the wind, till the seven continents and the seven seas were passed over, when they came to a green hill.

"I see," said the sheep, "that there the grass grows green and the pools are full of wine. What do you wish me to do?"

"At the bottom of the hill there is a black castle," said the maiden. "Go into that castle, and in each room stamp three times with your feet, and bleat once with your voice."

So the sheep went down the hill and found the castle. He went into the first room and stamped with his feet, and the echo ran through all the halls. Then he stamped a second and a third time. And then he bleated with his voice, and all the armor hanging on the walls rang. And presently he went into each room in turn, and when he came to the last one, and in each had stamped three times with his foot and bleated with his voice, suddenly the whole castle fell down and vanished like smoke, and the country it was on vanished, too, and he found himself back on the rock, where his brothers were nibbling the lichen and the moss.

"Brothers," he said, "I have had very strange adventures."

"Brother," they said, "you have never left this rock."

So a year went by, and the second sheep said:

"Brothers, I do not like this rock: I am going to look for a place where the rivers run with honey and bread grows on the trees."

So he climbed on to the plain, and he ran like the

wind for seven days and seven nights till he reached the Ivory Castle, and the same things happened to him that happened to the first sheep, and the king made him sit in the empty chair for a day and a month and a year, and two years, and ten years, and a hundred years: and then a great trumpet blew and a dwarf marched into the hall. He was very small, and had a hump on his back, and three horns on his head, and he was all black.

"Sir King," he cried, "grant me one of your men or one of your beasts to come with me."

So the sheep rose up and went with him.

"Where are you taking me?" he asked the dwarf.

"I am taking you into the center of the earth," said the dwarf.

No sooner had he spoken than the earth opened and swallowed up the dwarf and the sheep, too; and for three whole days and nights they fell through the darkness, till they came to a great cavern, where the fires that are in the center of the earth lick the roots of the mountains. And in the cavern were many other dwarfs, and each had a hammer, and was hammering a piece of brass into some shape or other. One was making an image of a man, and one of a dragon, and one of a sheep, and one of a cross, and one of a lion, and one was not making an image at all, but a machine for something or other.

"I do not see," said the sheep, "either rivers running with honey, or bread growing on trees: but what do you wish me to do?"

The dwarf led him to where the fires licked the roots

of the mountains, and there was a great glass cauldron full of molten brass set on the flames.

"You must leap into that cauldron," said the dwarf.

"But I shall be all burnt up," said the sheep.

"You will not," said the dwarf, and led him by his seven ribands to a high place from which he could jump into the cauldron, and then the sheep jumped. No sooner did he sink into the molten brass than the cauldron broke, and flames leapt up, tossing the sheep upon their points as if they had been a powerful fountain, and the earth opened above him, and presently he found himself on the rock where the other two sheep were nibbling lichen and moss.

"Brothers," he said, "I have had great adventures."

"Brother," they answered, "you have never left this rock."

So another year passed, and the third sheep said:

"I am tired of this rock. I will go where the birds blossom like flowers and the stars dance ring within ring."

So he climbed down on to the plain, and began to run like the wind, but not as the others had done towards the Ivory Castle. And after seven days and seven nights he came to a great river, very swift and very black. And floating down the river was a black boat, and in the black boat stood an old man, with a long white beard that reached down till it touched the water. When he saw the old man, the sheep felt that he must follow him; so he plunged into the river, and all that day they were swept along with the current, and with the evening the boat grounded in a shallow bay and the old man

stepped ashore, and the sheep landed also. Then the old man came and sat on the sheep's back and the sheep said:

"Smite me, Lord."

And he smote him with his hand.

Then the sheep began to gallop with him faster than the wind, and faster than the light of the sun: but presently he said:

"Lord, smite me again."

And the old man smote him again with the palm of his hand.

At that the sheep began to gallop and fly into the air, soaring on the speed of his galloping, till he had passed through the sky, and came where the birds blossomed like flowers, and the stars danced ring within ring. Then he said to the old man: "Let us rest here." But the old man smote him a third time with his hand, and at that all his strength went out of him, and he fell through the sky like a falling star, and dropped to earth like a plummet, right on the rock where the other two sheep were munching lichen and moss.

"Brothers," he cried, "I have had very strange adventures."

Then the other two sheep looked at him with surprise and anger.

"Brother," they said, "you have never left this rock."

ABOUT
THE
AUTHOR

Jeanne B. Hardendorff decided at the age of twelve to become a librarian and, after graduating from Southwestern in Memphis, attended Columbia University School of Library Service. Her career as a librarian has taken her to such places as St. Louis, Missouri, Muncie, Indiana, Baltimore, Maryland, and Brooklyn, New York.

Mrs. Hardendorff's career includes teaching children's literature and storytelling at the Graduate Library School of Pratt Institute in Brooklyn. She now lives in New Ipswich, New Hampshire, and devotes full time to her writing.